I0663115

Not Just My Mother's Daughter

Copyright © 2023 by Ivy Tobin, all rights reserved. No portion of this book may be reproduced in any form, scanned, stored or transmitted without written permission from Ivy Tobin and/or ThomasMax Publishing. An exception is granted for the quoting of brief passages for review purposes.

This book is a work of fiction, and all characters are products of the author's imagination. Any resemblance to real people, living or dead, is purely coincidental.

ISBN-13: 978-1-7377620-8-9
ISBN-10: 1-7377620-8-0

First printing, January 2024

Cover design by Ivy Tobin

Author photograph by David Vance © 2023

Published by:

ThomasMax Publishing
P.O. Box 250054
Atlanta, GA 30325

Not Just My Mother's Daughter

By Rose Gardner

ThomasMax
Your Publisher
For The 21st Century

*This book is in loving memory
of and dedicated to my mother.*

Acknowledgements

I am grateful for the creative inspiration provided by my family of origin: my parents, Sam and Sara and my sister Fern.

Many thanks and much love to my husband Harry for the countless hours spent editing my drafts. Your persistence and honesty sometimes caused arguments, but you never stopped pushing me forward.

A very special thank-you to my photographer and long-time, dear friend David Vance for creating my book cover.

Hugs and love to all those who inspired me during my writing process. You know who you are because we've been talking about this for years.

In loving memory of Ron Feinberg, my writing professor at The University of Miami and David Feldman, my high school drama teacher who always said, "If you knock on enough doors, one will open."

Special thanks to Lee Clevenger at ThomasMax Publishing for all your help and support making both novels a tangible reality.

A doormat would apologize for forgetting to acknowledge someone who influenced them. As the founding member of "The Society for Recovering Doormats" platform, with a global engagement of over 250,000 people, let me just say, if you feel offended, hurt or left out just know it wasn't intentional.

For all who've experienced the love and loss of your mother, this book reminds you that you're not alone. Whether you've actively participated in caring for a parent who was dying, or cared from afar, Not Just My Mother's Daughter *will bring you hope, encouragement, insight, and laughter.*

Praise for Not Just My Mother's Daughter

Mitch Poulos – Actor

Having lived the life of a struggling actor in the late 70s, 80s, and yes, part of the 90s, I could instantly relate to the main character in Rose Gardner's previous book "My Life as a Doormat". So having already bonded with the sweet, fun, quirky, loving Rose with all her idiosyncrasies, I was excited to go on another journey with her in "Not Just My Mother's Daughter". Turns out it was an unexpected voyage filled with raw honesty and humor as Rose conquers fears, faces childhood trauma, and questions life choices as she becomes the caregiver to her mother and a parent to her father. Amidst all of life's challenges, she still hangs on to hope as she searches to find her true self and along the way, learns to embrace her multifaceted relationship with her mother. The characters are beautifully written - complicated, multi-dimensional and the emotional ride you'll be taken on is universal and uplifting.

You don't have to have already read "My Life as a Doormat" to read this new book, but you'll definitely want to go back and do so afterwards. Rose's imperfections, struggles and dreams are something we can all relate to - and she's just too beautiful to let go.

* * * * *

Karen DeBonis – Author of *GROWTH: A Mother, Her Son, and the Brain Tumor They Survived*

While caring for her mother through her terminal illness, Rose Gardner comes to terms with childhood sexual trauma and family dysfunction. In the midst of the overwhelming demands of caregiving, she wrestles with her purpose in life. Ultimately, her mother's spirit guides Rose toward true love. A moving story of a mother-daughter relationship and the search for happiness.

* * * * *

Neda Leppard – Music Executive

I believe humor is birthed by observations and life experiences. Put that together with Rose and her cast of characters, an amalgamation of people we've known and loved, and people we've known and loved *not so much,* and you've got a real fun read that feels relatable and somewhat familiar. Can't help but feel a film or episodic series coming next!

Dr. Kristin Samuelson – Producer, Actor, Professor

Not Just My Mother's Daughter is a book that pulls you in from the first paragraph, everyone with a mother can connect with this story. A coming-of-age tale, written in a jaunty style that finds the comedic irony in difficulties of dealing with aging parents, you can't help identifying with Rose Gardner. Thoroughly thought provoking and entertaining at the same time.

* * * * *

Michelle Sulkin – Executive Marketing Director

The author creates a space to absorb the trauma of Rose by adding subtle humor to take the edge off of her difficult past. Viewing the situations through a comedic lens lends empathy to this story fraught with love and loss. A fast paced read taking a close look at the complicated relationship between a mother and daughter. Filled with quirky characters, and off-the-wall situations, *Not Just My Mother's Daughter* intrigued me from the get-go, and kept me engaged and entertained throughout.

Chapter 1

Family

My swift Manhattan departure seemed like months ago, but it was a mere three weeks earlier when I'd received the call. Awakened by my phone's loud ring at two o'clock in the morning, I substituted my thumbs for earplugs, but to no avail. The incessant noise intensified while I pulled the worn fleece blanket over my head and buried my face into my pillow. A moment later, Pirate Kitty cocooned on the nape of my neck and purred. We both knew the caller was a bearer of bad news. Catastrophic, terrible tidings always arrived in the wee hours of the morning. I'm not a clairvoyant, but it was Friday the 13th, the day designated for bad luck. Bad crap came in threes, and it had been one helluva week. A third disaster was imminent. The ringing stopped, and Pirate Kitty meowed, then jumped onto the floor.

"Feed me," his continuous meowing demanded. My stomach growled following him towards the kitchen while the phone rang again. Against my better judgment, I answered.

"It's Mom." Hearing Heather's voice on the other end of the phone completed the trifecta of unlucky events. "I'm at the emergency room! She couldn't catch her breath, so I dragged her to the hospital. They did a shit ton of tests, and the X-rays showed a huge mass on her lung."

My sister's voice, devoid of expression, sounded like she was giving a weather report. This news was hardly a surprise. Mom had smoked like a fiend for decades, and the dreaded anticipation of this inevitability always plagued me.

"They did an X-ray, and there's a huge mass," she repeated. "Mom thinks it's a mistake and she's convinced it's nothing." It was well after two a.m. This news had jolted me upright and wide awake. I knew I would be up for the rest of the night.

My mind raced as my sister rambled on. When I asked her to put Mom on the phone she said, "She's outside smoking in the parking lot. She's already talking about getting a second opinion 'cause she thinks the tech read the x-rays wrong."

Of course she thought it was a mistake. "Doctors are morons," she'd say. "What do medical tests prove, and what do doctors know?" Mom, the queen of denial, ignored or made excuses for everything, especially her health. She disliked all people affiliated with the medical field. "If they look hard enough, they'll find something. They need to make money, Rose. How else will they stay in business?"

Days before my move to New York City, (a decade ago) she'd coughed up blood and shrugged it off. She attributed her earth-shattering cough to postnasal drip. I suspected she knew something was very wrong, but Mom ignored my pleas to see a doctor and assured me (while convincing herself) she was in perfect health.

"Rose, you still there?" Numbed, I listened to more details pouring from my sister's mouth. "You should come home. Pack a lot of clothes 'cause you may wanna stick around a while."

Twelve hours later, on a plane headed back to my hometown in Miami, my head throbbed. My cat, inside the small animal carrying case, was sidled up next to me and mewed nonstop. "Get me out of here." His cries seemed to protest his entrapment, but maybe he was crying because he sensed the hell we were flying towards.

As I stared out the tiny airplane window into darkness, my emotional paralysis morphed into profound sadness. Tears drenched my face while I grabbed the animal carrier and headed to the lavatory.

It was the early '90s when plane bathrooms were a refuge for fighting spouses, the mile high club, and hysterical daughters whose moms were dying. A terrorist wearing filthy detonating shoes, locked inside an airplane bathroom wasn't yet a concept. I sat in silence on the closed toilet seat contemplating what I was going to say to her. Just as no one knocked on the lavatory door, no one noticed my empty seat in row twenty-two. I remained alone in my head, sequestered inside this charmingly smelly fortress. This familiar feeling of being invisible brought back my old mantra of *what next?* replaying on an endless audio loop inside my head.

"Ladies and gentlemen, we're now approaching our final descent into Miami International Airport," blared over the intercom, snapped me back to reality. My bones creaked as I stood up, opened the lavatory door, and began wobbling towards my seat, trying to shake off the fact that both of my legs had fallen asleep and cramped from sitting way too long in the tiny lavatorial enclosure. I was moving in slow motion, on unsteady legs, while tolerating being berated by the stewardess who insisted I immediately find my seat, sit down, and buckle up. A moment before the wheels hit the tarmac, I slid into my seat as Pirate Kitty's loud meowing was drowned out by the announcement of our flight's arrival.

Once inside the terminal and on autopilot, I spied the luggage carousel. Ten minutes later, with Pirate Kitty in tow, my suitcase was plopped into a large metal cart and maneuvered through the packed airport. It seemed forever before the exit doors leading to ground transportation appeared.

Outside, the thick night air was suffocating. I'd forgotten about Miami's heat and humidity as I grabbed a cab. Sweat dripped from my face while peeling off my coat inside the hot car reeking of stale cigar smoke. The twenty-minute ride felt endless, while the chain-smoking Cuban driver sped along Tamiami Trail. My eyes blurred seeing unfamiliar storefronts along this back road route to my parent's home.

"Are you headed in the right direction?" The driver didn't answer and increased his speed. The combo of cigar stench and his driving style was making me nauseated. With eyes closed, I sent out prayers to the universe to ensure the cabbie wasn't a kidnapper. A moment later, a cold sweat ensued while I took a deep breath and forced away *that* notion. *He doesn't speak English and misunderstood. He thought I'd asked him to speed up.* As if reading my mind, Pirate Kitty mewed in agreement.

A few minutes later, the cabbie turned right at the giant banyan tree adorning the far corner of my block. I wiped my sweat-drenched brow with the back of my hand as a wave of relief washed over me.

Home at last. My cat purred as the cab driver retrieved the suitcase from the trunk and sped away.

Crouching down and lifting the worn mat in front of the door took effort. My hand shook while retrieving the key from Dad's not-so-secret hiding place. Secret hiding place? My parents had endured five robberies in as many years, but my suggestions of a different place to conceal the key or installation of an alarm system fell on deaf ears.

The door squeaked and the unpleasant smell of cigarettes mixed with the scent of musty mildew wafted over me. My childhood home felt ancient. A small shade-less lamp stuck in the far corner of the living room threw creepy shadows upon the back wall. Taking a deep breath, I felt seventeen again, praying my parents wouldn't awaken while I snuck in past curfew. My plastic suitcase remained in the dimly lit living room while carting the cat case close to my chest. A loud meow was met with a "Shush" while tippy toeing down the narrow hallway towards my old bedroom.

After the door opened, fumbling in search of the light switch was next. A moment later the milk glass chandelier dangling over my bed flooded the room. Observing my new reality in the harsh light made me want to puke. Seeing the faded pastel wallpaper, a few stuffed animals and then feeling the unseen ghosts of my past was surreal. I felt trapped inside a time warp complete with my Iggy doll collection, incense burners, Teen Beat and TEEN magazines from 1973, which confirmed my feelings of being sucked through a wormhole back in time.

My geriatric cat's arthritis delayed his exit from the carrier. In human years he was over ninety and his movements were slow and deliberate. Once in go mode he wobbled over to the bed. His amber eye met mine, and I lifted him up. We huddled on top of the psychedelic flowered bed comforter. My high school yearbook, nestled beneath a stack of memorabilia beckoned, but looking through it would have to wait. As a result of several sleepless nights, exhaustion prevailed and my eyelids felt heavy while peeling back the bedspread. My body ached while thrashing around trying to get comfortable on the twin bed with the sagging mattress. My cat stretched out on top of me, a moment later my eyes shut, and we fell fast asleep.

The early morning sun streamed through the half-opened shutters while I stared at the ceiling.

"Rose, you sleeping all day?" Dad's gruff voice emitted from behind my bedroom door.

"Just getting up," I lied. Awake for hours and tucked beneath the hideaway of the bedsheets, I felt safe. My stomach tightened just hearing his voice. The thought of *seeing* my parents, especially Mom, filled me with dread.

Dad was no picnic, but at least *he* wasn't dying. Multiple cardiologists dismissed his imaginary heart condition, and the self-diagnosed brain tumor was deemed psychosomatic by several neurologists. His chest pains and fainting spells occurred only when he opposed something, (which was often) and couldn't have the last word. The year Mom packed her bags, and announced she wanted a divorce, Dad fainted and feigned a heart attack. Mom never left.

"I can't leave a sick man," she told her friends and endured several more years trapped within a miserable marriage. Although he'd announced his imminent death for years, Dad was still alive and kicking.

"I know you have a cat in there!" he barked. "I can smell it!' He laundry listed reasons for hating cats while Pirate's ears twitched. "Leave that stray in your room."

My stomach relaxed hearing his slippers shuffling away from behind my door. *Fuck you, Dad. Stray?* Pirate was more of a family member than him. STRAY? The audacity. I'd deluded myself into thinking he might've softened over the years, but he hadn't. "You're okay." Whispering reassurances and stroking my one-eyed companion helped me gain composure, but my shaking feline was smart, and knew he wasn't a welcomed guest. He leapt off the bed then stuck his paw underneath the door and hissed. His good eye darted back and forth from the closed door to me.

"Don't worry, you're safe." But even as the words tripped off my tongue, their validity was doubted.

When I was six years old, a kitten was left outside the front door of the apartment where we'd lived before moving into a house. Mom, very pregnant, was in the small kitchenette adjacent to the living room, waiting for a pot of wagon wheels pasta to boil.

Stretched out on our family room floor, engrossed with the television show *Mister Ed*, crying was heard. Outside, on the porch, was a calico kitten huddled inside a small basket. Attached to the side of the basket was a note scrawled in big block letters: "A GIFT FOR YOU."

"Mommy, someone left me a present." Squealing in disbelief and filled with joy, I picked up the tiny cat and cuddled her in my arms. "Why am I getting a gift? It's not my birthday or Chanukah". Holding the precious baby close to my chest with one arm, then opened the screen door with the other as Mom stood in the middle of the living room with a steaming bowl of pasta and bottle of ketchup.

"Whatcha got there, Rosie?"

"Look mommy, a kitten!" *Hadn't she heard me?* My arms stretched out towards her, confident she'd be excited, but her jaw dropped as she shook her head then told me the awful news.

"Dad hates cats," she said in a quiet voice.

"But this is a *baby* kitten not a cat," I pleaded to no avail. She explained how kittens grew up to be cats then restated Dad's disdain. It was the sixties, way before there was concern about cats being a negative health risk for pregnant woman, so of course she couldn't use that as an excuse not to keep her. Thus, Dad's dislike of cats came to the forefront and added yet another item onto my long list of things my Daddy wouldn't allow.

"Can I keep it *until* she's a cat?" She shook her head. "But she's a present!" I cried buckets and continued begging her to keep the kitten. She took my hand and led me over to the couch. We sat upon the overstuffed checkered sofa, while mom dried my tears with her apron. The kitten cried and mom got up, went into the kitchen, then returned a moment later with a bowl of milk.

"I'll talk to Dad when he gets home from work, but don't get your hopes up." She placed the bowl on the floor, and the little calico dove off my lap. My heart swelled, and I wondered if this is what true love felt like. "Don't worry. I'll see what I can do." Her words were soothing, but my anxiety issues already existed, and my sense of well-being wouldn't last for long.

Drifting off to sleep with the kitten cuddled up next to me felt wonderful but the next morning she was gone! Bewildered, my little feet charged towards my parent's room, but their bedroom door was shut. "Never come into our room when the door is closed!" My father's repeated reprimands echoed, and turning on my heels, I did a quick about face. Every inch of our tiny apartment was inspected with no luck. While crouched down and peering underneath the couch sounds of the screen door opening were heard. A moment later Dad's stern voice got my attention.

"Rose, if you're looking for that stray cat, it's not here anymore."

My eyes welled up. "Her name is Kitty Kit." Whimpering and choking back tears my eyes focused on the floor.

"I took the cat for a ride."

"To where?"

"Over to the canal by your school." *Why would he do that?* "Kittens need exercise and love to swim." He said, as if reading my mind.

"They do? Where's Kitty Kit now, is she drying off outside?" Hope sprang eternal while I ran to the screen door then searched the porch.

"She's not outside. She was enjoying the water so much I didn't want to rush her out. So…"

"You didn't leave her there?" Tears rolled down my cheeks as the blood drained from my face. "How will she get back?"

He told me cats found their way home. "If they want to." Dad smiled and the sadistic pleasure he derived from my pain was noted but not understood.

Obsessing over his words "Cat's come home if they want to," fueled my anxiety while waiting for the kitten's return. Everyday I'd place a bowl of milk outside the screen door hoping that today would be the day we'd be reunited. Then my sister was born, and we moved out of the tiny apartment into a house and hopes of our reunion ended forever.

Another knock on the door sent Pirate Kitty scurrying underneath the bed.

"Rosala, sweetheart, you up?' Mom's voice asked. A moment later the door swung open, and she stepped inside. "I'm so happy you're here," she repeated while holding on to me in a death grip. Surrendering inside her arms while holding back tears felt suffocating. A minute later she stepped back, and her deep-set brown eyes gave me a once over. "I don't like your hair that color." *Some things never changed.* "I'm so happy you're here," she reprised. Nodding my head while a forced smile crossed my face was all I could muster. I was unable to make eye contact, because if she saw the panic on my face, she'd ask a million questions. Questions I didn't want to answer. My head bowed as we walked out of my bedroom and headed for the kitchen. *Hold it together* repeated inside my head as I tried not to fall apart.

"The coffee is delicious." Mom smiled, then sipped from a chipped ceramic mug I'd made her in kindergarten. It had been a long time since we'd sat together at the old lime linoleum kitchen counter, and she picked up right where she'd left off. "I'm so glad you came home for a visit." *A visit? Was she delusional? Was she pretending to have no idea about the real reason I'd come home?* My strained smile remained intact because she lived in the world of *everything is fine* and displaying true emotions would make her uncomfortable. Fighting the apprehensive expressions that wanted to cross my face was exhausting. But succumbing to those feelings wasn't an option. For the first time in her life my mother needed me, (although she didn't know it yet) and if this charade helped her, then so be it.

My poker face remained in neutral while she told me I looked too thin, and feared anorexia was the cause. Then came the story about her friend's daughter who almost died from starvation. A moment later she reminded me about the tragic death of pop star Karen Carpenter. Every topic came with a minimum of three stories with zero time for comments. She recounted details about every person she'd ever known while I remained silent and squirmed in my seat. *How did she become an expert on other people's lives? I looked thin? (Well, maybe compared to her). And Karen Carpenter? I didn't even like her.* Mom smiled and savored her long sips of coffee and enjoyed every detail she spewed. Too much information about everyone; except herself. Skilled at avoidance, she didn't mention a word about the real reason I was there 'til the following day.

"You know Rosala, these crazy doctors saw something on my chest x-ray, and think I may be sick." Her eyes searched mine for support. She wanted me to jump on board her *denial express* and agree that doctors didn't know what they were talking about. But one of us had to be the adult and remain connected to reality. Just because I wouldn't jump onto her fantasy train, didn't mean I wouldn't slow it down a bit. "If they look hard enough, they'll find something." She shrugged. "Doctors! They're a bunch of thieves preying upon others' ignorance."

"They know more than we do, they went to medical school." I offered.

"Just because they have a diploma, I should trust them?" This was her opening parlay that would hopefully allow her to bail out of her upcoming doctor appointments scheduled for early the following week.

"Mom, we're going to the doctor's and hear what he has to say." She gave me a blank stare while I inhaled deeply and stepped into my big girl panties.

"They're all a bunch of money-hungry quacks! I think we should cancel those appointments. Doctors schmocktors, what do they know?" She pulled out a cigarette from a near empty pack then lit up.

"Mom!"

"Oh, sorry, you want one." *How could she be in such denial and unconcerned about her health? Did she really feel that way about doctors? Then why did she want me to marry one?*

"No thank you, I quit." Which of course was a lie. But how could I smoke in front of my mother who was dying of lung cancer? But maybe she wasn't dying, and I was the one overreacting. Perhaps she could have lung surgery, and she'd live another twenty years. Even if they needed to remove her entire lung, she only needed one to survive. How many lungs do you need to breath anyway? Perhaps that cancerous lung wasn't needed in the first place. My mind raced as I felt myself boarding mom's denial express.

Despite her reluctance, the following week found us driving to the doctors. "If it will make you feel better, then I'll go," she'd said half-heartedly.

My ride on her *denial express* was terminated when several x-rays and a biopsy all corroborated that things weren't looking good. "It appears to be inoperable lung cancer; however, we need to wait for all the test results to be processed to be sure." Despite the doctor's gloomy outlook, Mom was still convinced there was nothing wrong with her, certain that the entire medical industry was filled with con men. Late Friday afternoon, the call from the oncologist's office came confirming she had advanced, stage IV, inoperable lung cancer--two months to live without treatment, or maybe five with chemo.

I'd taken the call and knew the results would have to be edited. This information would need to be spoon-fed to Mom. She was still in denial and wouldn't want to know the details. (*Would she?*) I didn't tell her how long the doctors gave her, and she didn't ask. She agreed to the chemo only after I'd threatened to leave and go back to New York if she didn't at least give it a try.

And thus began our long debates about the pros and cons of her treatment. Of course, she had nothing positive to say and was still smoking like a chimney. "I think we can skip today, I feel fine," she'd announce. Every day was a struggle to get her to her appointments without a song and dance about what a waste of time it all was.

A few weeks later my life in Manhattan felt far away and non-existent. Back inside my old bedroom, the tiny black and white Zenith TV with the antennas covered in tin foil reminded me I wasn't in the Big Apple anymore. That ancient relic on top of my dresser, next to my Iggy doll collection drew me back to a familiar place, and soon it felt like I'd never even left home. One day blended into the next, and if not for my pocket day-minder I wouldn't have known what day it was.

No longer consumed by the grinding hustle of the City, this new reality of caring for Mom was my complete focus. No longer an aspiring artist, I was an unlicensed chauffeur driving Mom to doctor appointments and chemo treatments. I was an unlicensed nurse, wiping vomit off Mom's face and the floor. These activities replaced going to casting calls, being on film sets and attending acting classes. Her life was my life and took precedence while all thoughts about my past decade as a struggling actress were pushed into oblivion. My dad was caught up in his own imaginary health issues and couldn't deal with his wife's illness. Who knew? Turns out that the struggling artist, without any "real" career aspirations became the grounded, realistic adult in the family.

Despite her big mouth, Mom was a private person, and didn't want anyone hovering about and watching her die. "Rose is taking a leave of absence from New York" was her cover story. "Rose had a nervous breakdown," she'd explain to her friends and, without question, they believed that was the reason I was back home. "Rose is considering going to law school," she'd outright lie. But we both knew the truth. Mom might've told tales and played dumb, but she knew she was very ill. The grey pallor of her skin and the dullness in her eyes made the less-than-sterling quality of her health obvious.

I quit smoking, but Mom continued puffing away. Dad chased after her, ranting about the dangers of secondhand smoke and berated her, certain HE would contract lung cancer. "Some studies say it might be contagious," he continued while she cursed him underneath her breath.

When Mom wanted a smoke, she'd casually sneak out of the room. At first, her sneaky exits were ignored. But once I was smoke-free, like many ex-smokers, the smell of a lit cigarette became totally nauseating. As you might expect, my protests began. I'd become one of those obnoxious reformed smokers I promised I would never become. You know, the evangelical ex-smoker on a mission to eradicate the planet of cigarette smoke. But this was my Mom, and I wasn't going to let her accelerate the inevitable. What good was the chemo if she insisted on killing herself minute by minute, day by day? Sneezing and blowing my nose while following the thick trail of smoke emanating from beneath the closed den door was my daily routine. But this was getting old and being silent was no longer an option. My big girl panties intact, I prepared to rip the lid off Pandora's box and get rid of the elephant in the room. I was motivated to read her the riot act and stop at nothing to get her to stop this gaseous nonsense. I was ready to shout every empowering and motivating cliché I could think of. But when I opened the door and stepped into Mom's new smoking lounge, my mouth was unable to form words. Her eyes looked up at me with the vacant stare that accompanied her illness. Seeing her on the black faux leather couch, hunched over a small ashtray negated my power. Her vulnerability was palatable and filled me with sadness.

Her eyes refocused on the stream of thick smoke coming out of her mouth. "Look Rose, I'm gonna smoke whether you, Dad, or anyone else likes it. It's my one pleasure, and I already have the Big C, what else am I gonna get?" How could she be so dismissive and cavalier while I couldn't imagine losing my mommy? I felt deflated as tears flowed down my cheeks, and my extra-large, grown-ass woman's undies transformed into Pampers as I left the room and slammed the door behind me.

"I'm going for a walk," I shouted over my shoulder, then flung the front door open and ran outside.

Chapter 2

The Signs

Wheezing slowed my pace to a brisk walk. I looked down and noticed that the concrete sidewalk had splintered into a thousand spider webs and needed repair. But somehow, I'd navigated the path without stepping on a single crack. *Good job!* After patting myself on the back, a concrete corner stone that bore the street name caught my eye, so I plopped down upon the cement surface. *Breathe.* I gulped the thick humid air to fill my lungs and stop panting. *Why do I feel defeated and overwhelmed so soon? How am I gonna get through the next months? And why is this cornerstone so uncomfortable?* My eyes closed as my head throbbed. *Breathe.*

"Breathe." My therapist said. "It will help you with anxiety, Rose. Breathe deep and think of something that will make you feel grateful."

Gratitude. The concept rolled around inside my head for a long while. Being catapulted from my life and faced with the imminent loss of my mother had clouded my thinking. "There's always something to be grateful for." The therapist's words made me dig deeper and the aching inside my head began to subside. *I'm grateful to be away from Flo and her annoying sounds of hocking up phlegm.* Yes, Flo was a hocker. My current roommate had a nervous habit of constantly clearing her throat. It was mildly irritating at best and totally aggravating at worst. That is, irritating during the day and aggravating at night while I was trying to sleep. Wearing ear plugs helped, however, when she was awake her never-ending hocking was deafening. Referred by a roommate finder service, we were complete strangers when she first moved in. Initially, her "affliction" was barely noticeable. (Or perhaps my desperation for money to pay half the rent blinded me.) Living with more than ten roommates in just as many years, the bar was set very low as to what constituted an acceptable roomie. My tolerance level had strengthened and rendered me less picky and more broadminded about the string of misfits who resided inside my apartment.

Prior to Flo's arrival, an anal-retentive germaphobe who insisted on washing all the apartment walls called my place home. Before Mr. Clean, there was a gal whose alcoholic boyfriend slapped her around after drinking too much. When I finally got up the nerve to call the police and report the violence happening inside the next bedroom, she became furious. She told the cops at the front door there'd been a mistake and accused me of being jealous. She moved out shortly thereafter. She emptied out her closet and slammed the door without so much as a goodbye. *No good deed goes unpunished.*

At least Flo's boyfriend didn't beat her and never drank. When he offered to move in and cover my rent while I got things sorted out in Florida, my faith in humanity was restored. He was a solid person, almost saintly. Putting up with Flo's ongoing throat clearing was proof positive of that!

I'm grateful for Flo's boyfriend, what's-his-name. And just like that the pounding in my head was gone. I was calm now, but the feeling didn't last long as I flashed back on the conversation with my sister.

"You better come home and bring lots of clothes." Her words played in stereo. What she failed to mention was her departure from our parents' home, where she'd lived since graduating college.

"Your sister met someone and flew the coop." Dad told me this news update shortly after my arrival. Once again, Heather found the love of her life and took off on an extended road trip.

"She met him in a bar, and a week later packed a suitcase and left. Your sister is a slut, Rose." His beady hazel eyes bored through me. "That's why all of her relationships fail." My Dad, the person who thought cancer was contagious, was evidently also a relationship expert.

Facts were facts. Mom was dying, and I'd be caring for her alone plus dealing with Dad. This reality was of zero interest to Heather, as she'd tell you in her own words: "I can't be bothered."

As a kid, mom begged her to interact with other children. Her reluctance was strong because of her "what's in it for me?" attitude. She had developed advanced narcissistic skills at a very early age. She was a no-show at birthday parties, because, after all, she wasn't getting presents. "She's a shy child," mom would tell the questioning parents regarding her absence. Mom jumped to Heather's defense for years. When Dad repeatedly called my sister out on her freeloading, mom jumped to Heather's defense just like Pavlov's dogs. "She's finding herself," she'd said.

Dad reiterated that Heather was almost thirty, and after switching majors eleven times during her seven-year college escapade, it was time for her to be on her own. Or at least keep a job for more than two weeks. She'd graduated with a degree in finance but the only thing she'd used her degree for was pursuing a rich husband. She didn't feign embarrassment when I'd caught her practicing smiles in the bathroom mirror. She'd never leave the house without a full face of make-up on. Dressed in her too-tight clothing, she'd trot off to classes with little idea of what they were about. With no innate ability for math, she'd spent thousands of our parents' money for tutoring. After all, finance classes were where people learned how to make money, and she was interested in *those people.* So consumed with obtaining money, she'd had a few restraining orders issued for stalking potentially rich classmates.

"Not everyone has a plan or needs to be president of a corporation," Mom would explain without complaining about Heather's lack of direction, lack of skills, and gross lack of social graces. "I just want her to be happy" was mom's mantra.

Dad was indifferent to *anyone*'s happiness. All he wanted was Heather out of the house and off his payroll. "No more freeloading," he would emphatically state before walking out of the room. As usual, that was the last word.

Suddenly, I jumped off the concrete seat because my legs felt like they were on fire. Like a horror movie, red ants were crawling up my calves. I screamed while smacking them with the palm of my hand. "Holy fuuuuck." *What next, a rash? Locusts? How about a tornado?*

A little while later, I returned and stared at my childhood house, shrouded in overgrown weeds. My heart sank even further as the house looked even more depressing on the outside than it felt on the inside. The faded aqua paint was peeling, the roof sagged in the middle, and the faux brick trim along the window edges was chipped and outdated. The overgrown foliage covered the concrete walkway leading up to the front door, ending at an ancient straw mat with the word *WELCOME* nearly worn off. At another time, on another day, it might've felt more comical, like the Addams Family house, but today it felt much more ominous.

Step away from the house! Heeding my inner voice, I turned around and walked to the street corner near the end of the block. All of a sudden, the world got hazy and started moving in slow motion. I was drawn to this very spot like the accident you couldn't look away from. Vague echoes resounded in my head as the events that took place at the corner house, decades past, haunted me. The house, once an ordinary, non-descript one-story, had been knocked down and replaced. But this new construction didn't mask the truth of what had happened there years before. This replacement, a beautiful Spanish/Mediterranean style complete with a red clay roof and light grey painted walls, was very different than its predecessor, The brightly colored tiled entrance was warm and welcoming in dark contrast to the hostile events that had transpired on the property. The shed in the backyard was gone now, replaced by a swimming pool. But this beautiful new ambiance couldn't mask what occurred inside that rickety old shed all those years ago.

I would've dwelled on that childhood memory if not for being distracted by the *For Sale* sign displayed on the far end of the manicured lawn. Surprise replaced anxiety seeing my friend Mitch's face front and center on the real estate sign. Double-checking the name in bold letters below the picture confirmed any doubt. Yep, it was him! Mitch was in Miami too, selling houses. My astonishment pushed all memories about that childhood incident back into the dark recess of my mind, at least for the moment.

In the 80s Mitch and I were acting buddies. I hadn't thought about him for years, but now I couldn't STOP thinking about him. We were in the same scene study classes, practiced lines together and were each other's cheerleader as we pounded the Manhattan pavements in search of stardom. With his dark curly hair, and piercing blue eyes, I'd crushed on him big time. But like most of the men I fell for, he was gay.

He was a great friend, one of few people I could always count on. When I was cast in a play with an out-of-town road tour, he was there for me. He sensed that I was overwhelmed and offered to help sublet my apartment. "Perfect timing," he'd said, then elaborated about getting his real estate license as a side hustle. "It's a sign." He assured me it would be great practice for him to help sublet my apartment. If Ethan (my ex-boyfriend) hadn't come through and moved into my place, Mitch would've found the perfect person to sublet the space. *Had he turned his side hustle into a new career? I never thought he'd give up acting. What were the chances we'd both be in Miami?*

A side hustle is what we actors did while in-between gigs, but they seldom morphed into new careers. Back in the day, all struggling actors spewed random bullshit about leaving the business. Like the time going to nursing school crossed my mind, but my fear of blood made becoming a nurse impossible. Or the two days spent daydreaming about Mom's fantasy of me going to law school. But those were just passing considerations and were never acted upon. Giving up acting was a result of frustration but never a reality. It was hard to fathom Mitch as anything but an actor. Extraordinarily talented and disciplined, he loved the business more than anyone I knew. But here he was, a realtor in Miami. The sign proved it.

"It's a sign," I shouted to no one. *It's a sign* repeated inside my head while smiling back at his face beaming off the lacquered posterboard. After memorizing his contact info, I rushed home on a mission to find a pen and paper. What were the chances that my long-lost friend from New York City was right here in my own backyard in Florida? Floating on air as I wrote his number on a paper towel, I then tucked it inside my bra for safekeeping.

Thoughts about reconnecting with him lifted my cloud of gloom and doom. Now, for the first time in weeks, I felt like my old Manhattan self, ready to take on the world; if only for a moment.

Later that night I phoned my long-lost friend. He answered on the first ring. "I'm so happy to hear from you Rose," he repeated over and over. His enthusiasm quelched all previous doubts I'd had about making the call. Time and distance can sometimes have a negative effect on a previously thriving friendship but thank God this wasn't the case. "We have to get together as soon as possible," he'd said before our two-hour call ended. Filled with joy, excitement, and hope, I readily agreed.

Chapter 3

The Awakening

Sweat was dripping off my face. *Where am I?* After bolting upright, I felt trapped inside the world of my thirteen-year-old self. Lost in the inner recesses of my dreams, my breathing was labored.

"Mom, Heather won't leave me alone!" Silence. "Mom!" I screeched again. Eight-year-old Heather wasn't welcomed inside my thirteen-year-old world. "Mom!" I cried into the void. More pleas for help followed but she never appeared to rescue me from my little sister.

"Rose locked me out!" Heather wailed. The four-foot terrorist perched behind my bedroom door was intent on entering my personal space.

"She's so meeeeean!" Her fists continued pounding but no one came. I covered my ears and reeled from Heather's temper tantrum while guilt flooded within. Pirate Kitty licked my face, attempting to jolt me out of that dream, but it was a slow awakening. Drenched in sweat and in need of a shower, I headed to the bathroom.

The warm, pelting pressure felt life affirming as it washed away residual angst from my vivid nightmare. Afterwards, I pulled a T-shirt over my head, threw on sweatpants, grabbed the house key off my dresser and headed to the front door.

The moon was still in view as the sun rose from the east. Walking always cleared my mind. A few minutes later, I'd approached the end of the block. My feet froze while standing directly in front of the spot where I'd lost my childhood innocence. Being drawn here again, but this time in the wee hours of the morning, felt unsettling.

The perpetrator and his family had long since moved away, and their house had been demolished and replaced by a more contemporary-looking home. But the new house didn't erase the memories of what happened here on these less-than-hallowed grounds. At the time of the incident, I was but eight years old, incapable of comprehending this heinous event. It wouldn't be until years later that the assault on that warm spring day could be processed and understood.

"You're it," he'd said. Playing tag with my second-grade classmate, whom I secretly had a crush on, was a daily after-school occurrence. His yard was big and had a tire swing that hung from an ancient ficus tree. My classmate also had a teenage brother who hoovered around me even when we weren't playing tag. On this afternoon the brother asked me to come inside the old shed that sat on the back end of the property. "I want to show you something," he'd said. Young, naive, and trusting, I followed him inside, ignoring feelings of apprehension. My hesitation turned to panic as, once inside, he closed, then locked the shed door. He cornered me on the back wall and unzipped his pants. A moment later, he presented his penis and told me to kiss it. It was the first time I'd ever seen a male's privates and was dumbfounded. Knowing instinctively something was very wrong, I bolted away from him and tried opening the door. "Let me out," I screamed.

"Be quiet!" He ran behind me and used my ponytail to pull me onto him. Then the blackout occurred.

Unsure of how much time had passed when my eyes opened, my throat felt closed off. "Please let me out," I whimpered and noticed my shirt was unbuttoned.

"Shut up." He laughed and zipped up his pants. Once the shock subsided, my voice returned. I let out a blood curdling scream while he smirked then slowly unlocked the shed door.

"You've got a fat ass anyway. Who needs you?" These were his parting words while I buttoned up my shirt, then bolted out of the shed and ran home. For a long time, that is all I remembered about that day, but a nagging suspicion said there was much more I wasn't telling myself.

Feeling ashamed and embarrassed while being interrogated by my mom, I picked at my cuticles until my fingers bled. She knew I was upset, and it took a lot of coaxing, until I told her about the afternoon events. *Please don't be mad at me,* I prayed and avoided eye contact as my head lowered in shame. She was furious and the veins in her neck bulged while she ranted, then ordered me into my room.

"Never talk to that boy, or that family again!" She insisted but wouldn't answer my questions about why. Confused as tears poured down my face, I watched her leave the house through my bedroom window. Knowing she was going over to confront the brothers' parents filled me with dread. My whole world felt upside down and off kilter. *What did I do wrong?* She never answered my questions, but years later I understood why this childhood incident felt so demeaning and left me traumatized.

Since the father of the boy was a high-profile local official, no reprimand was given, other than the father's promise to talk to his teenager.

"Boys will be boys." His tone was arrogant and dismissive. He'd trivialized my mother's concerns, closing the front door in her face as if she were an unwelcome solicitor.

An eerie breeze snapped me back to reality as a chill traveled down my spine. I meandered back home, reassuring my eight-year-old self that I was fine. Neither the nightmare nor memories could have any power over me now. Diluting my strength by revisiting the past was not an option because I needed every ounce of energy to navigate the present. Mom needed my energy. It was my only way to move forward.

Days turned into weeks, as schlepping mom for chemo became my new normal. Every other week on Tuesdays and Fridays, we stepped inside her twelve-year-old Dodge Dart, with the plaid interior, temperamental air-conditioning, and no power steering. Mom backseat drove while we headed across town to the treatment center. She was an uncomfortable passenger. I'd driven for years but she provided irritating, unsolicited instruction. "You're driving too fast," she blurted out. "Speed up Rosala, you're like a turtle," came next. She gasped when I changed lanes, then slammed both palms onto the dashboard at the first sight of a stop sign, red light, or animal crossing. The faint sound of an ambulance sent her arms flailing. "Pull over."

I'd roll my eyes and bit my tongue. *Shut the hell up,* I'd scream inside my head.

Thirty minutes later, in a relieved but surprised voice she announced we'd made it, then opened her door and, at a snail's pace, exited the car.

I accompanied her inside the room with the twelve large, dark, reclining chairs. At first glance, it looked like a nail salon. The walls were painted a bright orange, and framed positive affirmations hung behind every chair. "I have already begun the healing process," "I deserve better health," "I trust the process of life to take care of me." Just a few uplifting thoughts from Louise Haye, the queen of positivity. This interior design attempt was intended to distract everyone from the real reason they were there. It failed. They could've had circus clowns, complete with acrobatics, filling the room and no one would be fooled. Everyone knew they weren't here for a mani-pedi. Even if the affirmations could distract us for a moment, the smell that permeated the room was a constant reminder of reality. The mix of cleaning products, illness, and fear, the spa had the foreboding smell of a floral scented mortuary.

The staff was pleasant, and Mom loved her nurses. She was an excellent cancer patient and never complained, even after several stabs into her ample arm to find a welcoming vein. After the tube delivering the poison was inserted, she'd settle into the big, brown, faux leather recliner and direct me downstairs to the hospital cafeteria. "Make sure they burn the fries, Rosala," she'd yell after me. French fries fetched, we'd sit side-by-side eating this comfort food until her sedative kicked in and numbed her reality. She'd fall asleep mid-treatment and I'd finish off her fries.

Her session ended and she remained half asleep as I helped her into a wheelchair. We left to a chorus of "have a good day" and "see you later" from the staff. Their cheerful sendoff didn't block out the visual of other patients receiving their treatments. *How many of mom's cancer colleagues would be at the spa next time?* Although there wasn't much social interaction between mom and her spa-mates, there was a strong feeling of camaraderie. A nod here, and a "how ya doing?" there, life affirming gestures that acknowledged fellow soldiers on the same side of a battlefield. All were comrades in arms fighting an enemy who would more than likely end their individual lives.

In the early nineties chemotherapy wasn't regarded as lifesaving, but rather life extending. "With chemotherapy, she's got five to six months," the oncologist told me in a cold, distant voice. Yep, it was the last-ditch attempt to prolong the life of a patient with stage 4 inoperable lung cancer. But even though the odds weren't good, maybe Mom could beat them! If she was still breathing and still complaining, there was a chance. I wasn't ready to relinquish my hopes and let Mom go because of the oncologist's pessimism. Hope sprang eternal.

I helped Mom, still groggy from her Ativan nap, into the car. She did no more backseat driving as she remained in a sedated stupor the entire ride home. Once inside the house however, the aftermath of the treatment began. It was non-stop vomiting, cursing, and cries of denial for the next three hours.

A few days later, Mom seemed back to her old/new self. She mentioned how she was going to turn Heather's room into an office once all this cancer stuff was over. "We'll repaint the walls a light shade of yellow and replace the shutters with drapes." Nodding my head, confirming her delusions, seemed the right thing to do. A minute later she reminded me how my hair looked brassy, and then came endless stories about more people whom I'd never met.

We hadn't spent this much time together in years. After college and before moving to New York City, we'd seen each other every day. Separation anxiety set in my first year away from home, but I didn't realize missing my mother was my problem (among others.) This epiphany was recent. Years of therapy revealed how focusing on all the abhorrent things about her was a coping mechanism that lessened my pain. If I'd succumbed to homesickness and my mother's constant pleas to return home, my Manhattan adventure wouldn't have lasted a week, let alone a decade. But there were times, like today, when my mother drove me batshit crazy.

It was a non-chemo day, so instead of the faux spa, we were seated at the white wicker table in our Florida room drinking endless cups of coffee. At mom's insistence, we were *not* talking about her condition. That painful subject was off limits. She chose to talk about me and cross my personal boundaries instead. Obviously, I needed to be embarrassed.

"How many sex partners have you had, Rosala?" She tapped her fingers on the table as I looked away. "I asked you a question, Rose!" A blank stare crossed my face while remaining silent. "I worry about you. If you're sleeping around, you could get one of those SPFs. Or even worse, AIDS."

"It's called STDs, and no, Mom, I'm not sleeping around so you don't need to worry."

She shook her head then continued her interrogation. Was I lesbian? And if not, why didn't I have a boyfriend?

She noted and named all my friends who were married, and then demanded a specific date when I would leave New York for good, come home, find a man, and settle down. "You're never going to find a husband in that crazy place."

A date that I would leave New York City? Was she serious? "I have my acting career. I can't just *leave*" Her dismissive attitude about my aspirations were infuriating.

"Waiting tables? Checking coats? *That's* an acting career?"

"That's just 'til the next acting gig." *Why do I waste my breath?*

"All that money spent on your college education." She shook her head. "At least if you'd met someone in school, it wouldn't have been such a waste of our finances." She paused for a moment and reloaded her ammunition. "I want grandchildren, Rose! Did you ever stop to think about me?"

Feeling attacked, I wanted to blurt out, *what difference does it make, you won't live to see them.* But held back. "It's my life!" My body stiffened, and my ears rang.

"Rosala, you're over thirty and statistics prove girls your age have a better chance of getting struck by lightning then getting married." She lit up a cigarette, then inhaled deeply. Her inappropriate intrusiveness rattled me, so I changed the subject.

"Mom, don't you think you should *try* to quit smoking?" She didn't answer but gave me a long hard stare.

"Sometimes I think it's my fault you're alone." Another uncomfortable conversation was about to unfold. "I should've taken you to a psychiatrist after--"

"That was a long time ago. It doesn't matter." My neck stiffened.

"It does matter! That boy should've been arrested," she persisted.

Those deep buried memories, suddenly unearthed during my return home frightened me. "Please, I don't want to talk about this." I pleaded.

"Maybe if I'd reported him to the police, instead of just--"

"STOP. Enough, Mom." But my words fell on deaf ears.

"Why didn't his parents do something? I should've gone to the authorities."

Could've, should've, would've were the words she lived by.

"What happened has nothing to do with why I haven't met anyone," I said, hoping that would end the conversation. But no, she persisted.

"If only I'd known what to do, maybe you wouldn't be so afraid to have a meaningful relationship." Her eyebrows arched.

"Getting married and having kids isn't for everyone." She ignored me.

"It would be a shame for you to end up alone. Or even worse, with five cats." A single tear rolled down her cheek. "I hate seeing you waste your life." And there it was. She viewed me as a failure. According to her, anything short of having a husband and child made me a loser. *Look at your own life, Mom*! *Did staying in a miserable marriage validate and fulfill you?* Her thoughts were a whole new level of old school antiquated, but mentioning that would only extend a conversation that I wanted over. Besides, I couldn't yell at a dying woman.

"You're right mom," I acquiesced, kissing her on the cheek before walking back to my room with a throbbing headache.

It was during those conversations with Mom when my gratitude for Mitch being in Florida grew. We'd talked several times since I'd reached out and he was always upbeat and caring. I'd been counting the days until our meet up. The date was circled in red on my calendar, and tomorrow was the day! Our day! I held the paper calendar close to my chest and knew tomorrow couldn't come fast enough!

Chapter 4

Bridges

Thursday morning, seated behind the steering wheel of my
mother's car felt empowering. Finally, a day just for myself! But the
traffic was heavy, and the trip was now delayed. Sitting in traffic, my
eyelids drooped and the taunting voices of children singing, mixed
with vicious laughter filled my head. It was a memory from the
aftermath of the shed incident still haunting me. The children chanted
"Rosie Posy Pumpkin Pie kissed the boys and made them cry." Shame
and being frozen by fear prevented any rebuttal.

Facts were fictionalized as rumors spread around town. The
overzealous eight-year-old girl was labeled as the aggressor and the
young teen boy, the victim. Dehumanized, I was treated like a pariah.
Parental conversations that should've been private, held behind
closed doors, weren't. Children often repeat what they don't
understand, and their comments initiated years of endless bullying.
The humiliation of their mean-spirited taunts chipped away at my
already low self-esteem.

A horn blared and returned me to reality while that disturbing
recollection was shoved back into the inner recesses of my mind.
Breathe. Now wasn't the time for analytical retrospection of that
trauma or self-therapy. Crossing the drawbridge connecting
downtown Miami with Miami Beach was moments away and needed
my full attention. The deep-seated fear of driving over bridges would
make this challenging, and the dauting task took precedent over
anything else. I took another deep breath and soldiered on.

"Let's meet at the bus bench in front of *The News Café* at two-thirty for a late lunch," Mitch suggested on the phone. When I recommended another meeting place that didn't entail crossing bridges he balked, then repeated the address. He was adamant about the location. As a longtime friend, he knew all about my phobias and I wondered why he was so inflexible.

"I have a surprise waiting for you there." Now my campaigning for a change of venue was futile, and as if reading my mind, he said, "If you're nervous about driving over the bridge, then take the bus."

Maybe I'll conquer my fear of crossing bridges after all! My hopefulness lasted until the bridge was in sight. The sweating began and the sense of foreboding surged upon me, seeing the flashing red bridge lights in the distance. The bridge was going up. The sweat started dripping from the nape of my neck down my back. My clammy hands were over-gripping the steering wheel as I contemplated turning back. But since I was also afraid of making U-turns, I was trapped. My stomach flip-flopped as I stomped on the brakes with both feet, guaranteeing my car would remain immobile. Eyes closed, I counted out loud, employing a useful coping skill I once learned from a therapist. My breathing slowed. "Two hundred and twenty-seven," I said as the echoing blast of car horns from behind alerted me the bridge was down, at last. It was time to move. *Well done*. Mentally patting myself on the back, I continued with the challenge of traveling over the bridge. *I can do this*, I reaffirmed, removing both feet off the brake.

Fifteen minutes later, the car was parked on a narrow side street. My shoes pinched walking a long block to the main drag. The buildings along Ocean Drive were once hotels and apartments where old people lived out the latter days of their lives. When my grandfather resided there, the area was referred to as God's Waiting Room. Now God was evidently offering nouveau cuisine at newly converted trendy restaurants. Tourists were staying at upgraded deco hotels, clothing boutiques sold the newest designs in haute couture and, of course, there were headshops selling bongs, power hitters, and rolling papers.

This was not my granddad's South Beach. Except for the hotel reconstructions repainted in tropical colors, the buildings all looked the same as they did back in the day, but the vibe was completely different. Instead of being demolished, these old dwellings had been refurbished, and many were deemed historic landmarks. The signage was poor, and South Beach's significant metamorphosis felt overwhelming. *Where the hell am I?* Lost, yes lost and couldn't find the restaurant. Perhaps I'm on the wrong South Beach? But how many South Beaches were there?

A few minutes later, the tiny sign for the restaurant appeared. Flooded with relief, I caught my breath and turned onto a pathway. "Rose!" Mitch's voice yelled out as he waved, then ran up the gravel-covered walk. Within moments, we were wrapped in each other's arms.

After the initial excitement of our reunion subsided, all angst about crossing bridges faded. I looked into my handsome friend's sapphire blue eyes and smiled. "Where's my surprise?"

He didn't say a word but grasped my hand as we walked a few steps towards the restaurant. Then he stopped and pointed to a bus bench. "This is it!" His grin was returned with my blank stare.

"What about this?"

His eyes sparkled and he seemed amused by my confusion while tucking me underneath his arm, then led me around to the front of the bench. "The camera got my good side." He was pointing at his larger-than-life face, supplemented with a real estate logo, covering the bench. "Hey, if I can't be a star on Broadway with my mug on a marquee, then this will have to do."

He was beaming, seemingly elated with his new profession and I wondered if anything other than acting could bring me that magnitude of joy. Mitch was such a dedicated, brilliant actor, and so devoted to the business. This career change was mind boggling, but he appeared happy giving showbiz the boot. Outwardly, he seemed fulfilled gaining recognition from a bus bench, but my gut feeling told me he wasn't.

A few minutes later we were seated across from each other in this trendy South Beach eatery. Seeing him outside of New York City felt surreal at first, but it wasn't long until the odd feeling disappeared, and the comfort only close friendships could share returned. Within minutes, it was as if we'd seen each other yesterday.

We ordered BLTs and two glasses of chardonnay from the tall, thin waiter. I wasn't Kosher, but seldom ate bacon because eating pure fat was disgusting! But Mitch insisted the BLTs were to die for. I didn't want to die but ordered it anyway.

The waiter took the menus off the table, and then left us alone to catch up on lost time.

"I think our last visit was when we met up at The White Horse in the--" Mitch offered up as I cut him off.

"No, because you helped me sublet my apartment, and that was a few months afterwards."

"Maybe it was at that open audition for *Romeo and Juliet* in--" he interjected.

"No, for sure it wasn't then. I never auditioned for that." It was hard not over-talking each other as the memories flooded back. I was the worst offender and noticed Mitch's concerted effort allowing me to finish my sentences. He was a polite and gracious person and didn't say a word while my mouth blabbered on. He let me jabber away while he smiled and nodded. A half hour into our visit we still couldn't figure out how long it had been since we'd seen each other.

"Does it matter?" Mitch asked as our waiter arrived with the food and offered up another drink. He ordered vodka on the rocks. Challenged enough driving sober, I declined.

"We're here *now*." He said as the waiter left. We knew it had been far too long and agreed to leave it at that.

"I wonder what ever happened to Stephen?" he said after biting into the overstuffed sandwich.

"Our acting teacher?"

"How many Stephen's with a "PH" do you know, Rose? Yes, of course our old acting teacher."

I hadn't been to acting class in more than three years but had heard interesting gossip. "I'm not sure but there are rumors that he's had… surgery."

"A facelift? Appendix? Tummy-tuck?"

"No, he bought breasts." Mitch's jaw dropped. The words felt strange coming out of my mouth. Sexual transitioning was unusual during the nineties. We were decades away from the LGBTQIA revolution. Gender choices, and sexual fluidity weren't commonplace, even in the acting community, and the option of using pronouns other than the sex you were assigned at birth didn't exist. There was only he/him, and she/her. They/them was around but used very differently back then. Closeted gays referred to their same sex partners as they, trying to conceal their gender identity. It would be thirty years in the future before same sex couples were granted the right to wed. The nineties was a more conservative time and even most professional NYC drag queens opted for a less permanent commitment to womanhood. And Stephen wasn't even a drag queen. He was a conservative acting teacher who had studied theater arts at Yale. His wardrobe consisted of denim jeans paired with a blue and white check patterned shirt. *Always.* Short sleeves for summer and long sleeves during the winter. "It's just a rumor." My eyes twinkled as I took a fry off his plate then covered it with ketchup.

The waiter returned and set Mitch's drink next to him. He finished the last drop of wine then handed the waiter the empty wine glass.

I picked up the vodka and took a sip.

"Do you think he wears blue and white checked gingham dresses instead of those shirts?" He teased.

I closed my eyes and tried imagining Stephen's closet filled with five identical dresses all hung up and spaced ten inches apart.

"Maybe he changed his name from Stephen with a "PH" to Stephanie.

"Yes, Stephanie with a PH." I added.

Laughter ensued and Mitch continued. "Or better yet, "Stella," he shrieked, then downed the rest of his drink and called out again. This time even louder. "Stella, Stellllla," he wailed. Our behavior would be considered politically incorrect by today's standards, but back in those days political correctness wasn't yet a *thing*.

True, Stephen had always been a fan of *A Streetcar Named Desire,* so Stella made more sense than Stephanie. "I've always counted on the kindness of strangers." I played along. My southern accent sucked, and Tennessee Williams would be rolling in his grave.

His outcry got the attention of our waiter. "Another drink, sir?"

He nodded then handed the waiter his empty glass.

"For me too. Vodka on the rocks, please." I piped up then opened my BLT, removed all the bacon and placed it on Mitch's plate. He devoured it while my sandwich remained half eaten and mutilated beyond recognition. A few moments later my drink arrived. "Cheers!" Clinking our glasses solidified our celebration.

"Rose, if you can't drive home, I'll get you a cab." Mitch offered.

"I'm fine with that drawbridge," I assured him.

"I wasn't referring to the bridge." Pointing to the drink in my left hand, his eyes narrowed, and his brow furrowed like a disapproving mother hen. His concern was touching, but my promise to drink lots of coffee before driving eased his worry.

"Pinky swear?" He extended his little finger.

"Pinky swear." Wrapping my finger inside his felt comforting.

Four hours and three cups of strong coffee later, he walked me to my car. "You sure you're okay to drive?"

After five minutes of reassurance, he opened my car door, kissed me on the cheek and sent me on my way.

The smell of cigarettes prevailed while opening the front door. It had been this way for as long as I could remember. My heart sank seeing my mother perched on the living room couch, like a panther waiting to pounce upon their prey. "Where were you?"

I walked through the living room then stowed my purse on a nearby chair. "South Beach."

"You drove over *that* bridge? Rosala, I'm so proud of you." I was standing instead of sitting in the chair because sitting down ensured I'd be trapped.

"Come, sit with me for a little while." She patted the couch cushion next to her, but I remained standing.

"Why did you schlep all the way to South Beach?"

"I wanted to walk on the beach." I lied.

Her eyebrows arched and her worried look changed to disapproval. "Why did you run off without telling me *where*? Are you hungry? You walked on the beach wearing those shoes? I hope they didn't cause a blister." Nothing was a bigger buzz kill than mom giving me the third, fourth and fifth degree. Several more questions followed, as I weaved and bobbed, keeping my responses short and vague.

"I was alone." This lie would derail further questions. Especially her inquiry of who I was with.

"Alone?" She looked surprised and a second later I grabbed my purse off the chair and said goodnight. Lying wasn't my strong suit, but if I'd told her the truth that would've caused an avalanche of even more questions.

"What's his name?" she'd ask. Then, "what does he do for a living?" And of course, "are you gonna see him again?" Inappropriate, irritating questions that were none of her damn business. I was a grown woman and didn't have to answer to my mother. Just because she treated me like a little girl didn't mean I had to comply. (Did it?)

Once sequestered inside my bedroom I called Mitch and he sounded relieved my car hadn't careened over the side of the bridge or smashed into another vehicle. *Didn't anyone have faith in my driving skills*? (Maybe they shouldn't?) Our reunion on South Beach started my new normal -- speaking with Mitch every day. It made taking care of Mom a lot easier.

Chapter 5

Today is Not That Day

By mid-May, Mom's medical routine was down pat. Her chemo treatments, her follow-ups, and my private chats with her oncologist were regular events. He assured me x-rays didn't lie, and her prognosis wasn't good. He handed me three business cards of people and places to contact for additional help. "You're going to need it." His tone was matter-of-fact.

I felt dispensable and threatened. Overseeing mom's life was *my job* and had bestowed a new sense of purpose previously lacking during my past years in New York City. Despite my goal to be a working actor, most of my time was spent otherwise. There were endless days chasing opportunities to get acting jobs. The auditions and casting calls that resulted in disappointment. I hated the cattle calls where hundreds of actors would show up striving for an opportunity to be seen and get selected for the one available role. It was completely demeaning. Thousands of rejections for reasons unknown. At the same time, I was actively engaged in a multitude of acting classes and workshops to keep my skills sharp as I prepared for the random acting job that drifted my way. Exhausted from juggling waitress shifts, temp jobs and coat checking gigs to finance my dream left me unfulfilled and doubtful. Most days I felt invisible and wondered what the hell I was even doing there!

I am all the help my mom needs, and no one is going to replace me, especially not strangers from health care agencies. Ignoring the doctors' referrals, I crumpled up the cards and threw them into a wastepaper basket near his desk.

"What did the doctor say?" Mom whispered on the drive home.

"You're doing great," I lied. Now, a permanent resident in her land of denial, I halfway believed the untruths rolling off my tongue.

A few minutes later, we arrived home, walked through the front door and heard Dad's slippers shuffling on the terrazzo floor inside the kitchen. "Heather called and needs money." He bellowed. "She's broke." These were the first words out of his mouth. Not "hello" or asking how mom's doctor visit went. "Heather called!" He repeated as mom proceeded to the living room couch then sat down.

At first, Heather's convenient departure had pissed me off. But now gratitude replaced anger. In hindsight, her presence would've been a giant pain in my ass. She also was a hypochondriac, like Dad, and her non-participation in what should've been a family affair would've only hindered things. Her running off with the stranger from that bar was indeed a lucky break. If she'd stuck around, I'd be taking care of one cancer patient and two hypochondriacs. One was enough.

My sister's tremendous fear of illness began in childhood. At four years old she'd experienced a mild case of chicken pox and asked our mom if she was going to die. Mom reassured her she'd be fine, but Dad wasn't as comforting. He shook his head then shared a story with Mom about his childhood friend that had died from the disease, complete with graphic details about his comrade's suffering and demise and all within earshot of her young, naïve ears. And mine.

Dad, like Mom, had trust issues with doctors, in addition to being a tightwad who resented paying their inflated medical charges. Having medical insurance wasn't the norm during our childhood, so we didn't have any. Not seeing a board-certified doctor left only one other option: a veterinarian. Not just a random animal doctor, the vet we saw worked at the racetrack where Dad had his haberdashery. This Doctor Dolittle was highly respected by jockeys and horse trainers. And of course, Dad.

"I don't want the kids going to that quack," Mom raged.

Our dad assured her that the man went to a very fine husbandry college. "He has as much medical training as those shyster doctors charging an arm and a leg." His bartering system, merchandise for medical treatments, ensured the visits would be cost effective.

Heather, always sick with a cold or sinus infection, allergies, headaches, and a self-diagnosed irregular heartbeat, reminded me of Dad. You name it, and she thought she had it. She searched for the best doctors, specialists, and top shelf medications for the countless illnesses' resident only inside of her head. And just like Dad, Heather thought cancer was contagious. She was her *father's* daughter. A hypochondriac clone.

"Where is she? How is she? Does she still have that boyfriend?" Not waiting for Dad's answers, she fired off one question after another until she was out of steam. It was hard discerning whether it was the cancer or concern causing her shortness of breath. She'd been anxious since Heather fell off the radar and expressed her apprehension daily.

"We'll hear from her when she needs money," Dad reassured her and added, "No news is good news." And true to his word, Heather resurfaced the moment her cash flow dried up.

"But we know nothing about the man she's with. He could be a criminal or even worse, a murderer!" Mom protested.

"She sure knows how to pick 'em," Dad mumbled.

"What if he's doing drugs and gets her hooked on heroin?" Mom pleaded.

"Drugs, schmugs. Being with this guy is cheaper than her living in my house. I hope he keeps her and doesn't bring her back," Dad shouted.

"How can you be so lackadaisical about our child's safety?" She began coughing while Dad talked over her gagging sounds.

"She's somewhere out in Arizona. That's where she asked me to send her the money." Then, as an afterthought, "She sounds fine."

"Didn't you ask her what she's doing?" Mom whispered.

"She's doing the same crap she did here. Nothing."

"But did you *ask* her?"

Dad was dismissive and didn't answer mom's question. "I have a P.O. box number to send the check to." He shuffled off to the nearby desk where he kept the check book.

Mom's coughing returned full force, so I left the war zone to grab her a glass of water from the kitchen.

After a few sips, her hacking subsided. Moments later, Dad returned. "We're out of stamps!" He raged and waved the envelope in mom's face.

"Did she leave a phone number?" Her hoarse voice quivered. He turned his back on her, then headed to their bedroom. Mom's coughing resumed and it took several gulps of water before it subsided and her breathing returned to normal. Several minutes later, she composed herself and got off the couch.

"I can't believe this man!" She murmured underneath her breath, shook her head, then headed to the den for a smoke.

I retreated to my room, then stretched out on top of the bed. Pirate Kitty meowed at my bedside. He wanted to join me but couldn't manage the jump from the floor to the mattress. Watching his failed attempts to get next to me was heartbreaking, so I reached down and scooped him up. He purred while being positioned on the center of my stomach. His exact age was unknown, but he was old. Really old. A sudden wave of sadness washed over me while petting my beloved feline. "Don't you die too." Tears flowed then turned into sobs. And, in a blink, my sixteen-year-old-self returned. Hysterical crying during my teenager years, on this same bedspread, was commonplace. My youth was a cliché with a side of continuous drama. If I'd known then what I knew now, I'd explain to my confused teenaged self how my angst was hormonal, and all teenage girls hated their mothers. Truth be told, it wasn't loathing, just intense resentment.

"Mom! I'm almost eighteen! Why do I need a curfew?" I'd flinch while she reminded me that I was only sixteen, then insisted there wasn't a rush to grow up.

"Enjoy your youth as long as possible," she repeated and assured me adulthood wasn't all it was cracked up to be. Another thing I wished I'd believed and would've told my teenage self. But back then, I wanted to do what I wanted to do, but she was the gatekeeper of my freedom. At sixteen everything was an emergency and needed immediate approval and compliance.

"Don't you trust me?" My eyes squinted, while digging in my heels, determined to have my way.

"Trust has nothing to do with it." A silent stare-down followed, and her light brown eyes emanated tremendous sadness. I didn't understand why my mother's eyes looked like those of a lost puppy but was certain it had to be my fault. And so, I'd back down on my campaign for freedom. "Okay," I whispered and hung my head in defeat. She left the bedroom and closed the door behind her. Bursting into tears always followed her departure.

A knock on the door jolted me back to reality and then Dad's voice blared through. "I can smell that kitty litter from down the hallway!" Then his threats: "If I smell that goddamn cat shit one more time, I'm taking it for a long ride."

At that singular moment an epiphany occurred. The sadness that prevailed in mom's eyes had nothing to do with me, but everything to do with him.

By the second week of June, Mom's illness was more apparent. Her rapid decline was most evident during the car rides to her chemo appointments. When the sunlight hit her face, her once olive complexion looked grey and sometimes jaundiced. She had the pallor of someone who was living on borrowed time. Warnings of this reality and to *prepare* fell on my deafened ears. *How do you prepare for losing your mother?* This inevitability was unfathomable. Someday I'd have to face losing her, but *today* was not that day. I blasted the radio and, to no avail, attempted to block out these thoughts.

"I'm thinking of re-wallpapering Heather's bedroom. Something new and fresh for when she gets back." Apparently, she'd ditched the idea of turning my sister's room into an office. Ever since she'd called, Mom assumed Heather would come home soon, and life would proceed as normal. Or at least normal-ish. She'd made light of the tremendous changes bombarding her life, and now placating Mom's reality was my standard behavior.

Stopped at a red light, tilting my head in her direction, our eyes met, and I caught a glimpse of her smiling. "That sounds great." Tears welled up in my eyes as the light changed and forced me to get a grip!

The storm clouds rolled in as we parked the car then walked inside the building. Too proud, vain, and in denial, she wouldn't agree to a wheelchair and insisted on walking despite the tremendous pain crippling her body.

Thunder sounded as we rode the elevator to the third floor. A few moments later she was situated in her chair, and I walked out into the waiting room and sat down in a nearby chair. Peering out of the enormous picture window, watching the storm clouds gather, large flashes of lightning lit up an otherwise black sky. It felt comforting. There was something soothing, almost reassuring about these afternoon downpours. They showed up every day like clockwork and reminded me that some things never changed, and life would continue to go on, no matter what.

Isolated inside the empty waiting room, watching the storm was hypnotic. Closing my eyes, random thoughts filtered through my head and reminded me of an emotional storm from years past. A few minutes later, as I was half asleep, my best friend Jules appeared. We'd been joined at the hip since kindergarten. It was a rainy afternoon, and we were two nine-year-olds walking home from school sharing a single umbrella. We heard footsteps approaching but ignored them. Then came the push from behind, jolting me out from underneath the safety of the umbrella and knocking me to my knees.

"Rosy Posy," the girls chanted. The bullies, both named Nancy, were the cool kids from our elementary school. If you weren't in their clique, be afraid. Be very afraid. These two cornered me on the ground in front of a deserted gas station. The bigger Nancy pinned me down, as the smaller one grabbed my handbag. Before I'd realized what had happened the two bolted off with my purse and were heard laughing five hundred yards ahead of us.

"Rose, you okay?" A stunned Jules helped me to my feet. We both cried and hugged each other, as a gust of wind turned the umbrella inside out and carried it away.

"You're drenched!" Mom's face scowled when I walked through the door. "And you're late." Before I'd had a chance to explain, she was off on a tangent about how nervous she'd been and starting tomorrow I'd have to take the bus. "No more walking home from school," she shrieked. After her tirade, a fresh bout of tears arose. All color drained from her face as I told her every detail about the incident with the two Nancys. "Never to talk to those two girls again!" She pulled me close to her. *Never talk to them again.* The same advice she'd given me about the neighborhood boy a year earlier. Reporting bullies to the authorities wasn't a concept back in the 1960s. My mom did what all the other moms of nice girls did: nothing. She told me nice girls don't fight back. Instead, they ignored mean people. What she neglected to say was that not fighting back and standing up for myself would be very costly. Being too nice had an extraordinarily high price tag called damaged self-esteem.

Now fast asleep, the gentle nudge of a nurse awoke me. My eyes popped open as my body spasmed then jolted out of the chair. "Your mom is done with her treatment." She smiled then walked out of the waiting room, while I was still in a fog, I tried recollecting myself while trailing behind her.

A half hour later, we were inside the car driving home. The storm was over, and a vibrant rainbow stretched across the sky. Mom slept during most of the ride, which was good because the soaking wet nine-year-old buried deep inside me was still weeping.

Chapter 6

Not Just My Mother's Daughter

A few days later, seated in a front booth at Sambos, my neck stiffened while I contemplated purchasing a pack of cigarettes. Anxiety ridden, perhaps a few puffs would calm my nerves. *I could buy a pack, take two or three out, and then throw the rest away.* I bargained with myself while waiting for Mitch and looked at the vending machine located near the hostess station. "BUY ME," the Marlboro 100 Lights beckoned. *What harm would one or two puffs do?* Smoking in public places was permitted in the 90s. Hell, no one cared where you smoked nor gave a thought to the racist branding of the popular restaurant chain, Sambos. The racial slur for a loyal and contented black servant was an acceptable name for this place serving endless cups of coffee on Miracle Mile. Most people were more concerned about Julia Roberts films and Michael Bolton's music than bigotry, political correctness, or the effects of smoking and secondhand smoke.

Temptation won out and my back ached while stooped in front of the machine, rummaging through my purse for coins.

"Caught you!" Mitch's voice boomed from behind. My face flushed while turning around to face him.

"I haven't bought them yet. You showed up in the nick of time." A dramatic bow followed. "My savior."

"You mean in the nick-otine." He hugged me and I forgot all about caving into my craving.

"How'd the showing go?" The house he was selling was where I'd been assaulted, but I kept that factoid to myself. Seated across the booth from him, the oil slick on the tabletop made me cringe. Retrieving several napkins, I wiped away the filth while Mitch spoke. His familiar voice felt comforting.

"The couple I showed that old house to, the one at the end of your block, seemed interested." Dressed in a tan blazer, complete with a pale blue button-down dress shirt, tie, and tan linen pants, it was difficult not to gawk.

"You look so professional, like a top-rate realtor." He could've been a movie star.

"Gotta dress the part." Fidgeting, he opened the menu and a moment later, his tone of voice changed. "C'mon Rose, we both know we'd rather be acting." His lighthearted demeanor grew somber. "But I couldn't take it anymore. The rejections and being poor." Hiding behind the menu he continued. "Sick of the freezing winters, I wanna enjoy the year-round summers in Florida." He recounted more reasons for leaving the entertainment industry, sounding apologetic for quitting show biz and leaving New York City. "For the first time in my life I have a savings account and a tan." He faked a laugh. "But I totally sold out." His tone was confessional as he shook his head and laid the menu on the table.

"No, you didn't sell out! You made a successful career change and I'm proud of you." Truth was, I was very proud of him, and sad that my gut feeling was right. His ecstatic behavior about being featured on a bus bench instead of on a marquee was all an act. Now, knowing he was secretly miserable was soul crushing. Our eyes met and his baby blues smiled, but his mouth remained taut. "One of my old roommates decided acting wasn't for her and became a doctor. She was sent over to Africa and worked with Doctors Without Borders. You're not the only one to bail on the biz." What I didn't tell him was she'd been hit by an ambulance while leaving a hospital after a night shift. She lingered in a coma for five weeks and died.

The waitress showed up and took our orders. "More coffee please, and a tuna sandwich." I handed her my menu.

Mitch ordered a Tab. "I binged on doughnuts at the showing. Gotta keep my girlish figure." He patted his stomach then laughed as the waitress, apparently not delighted with her career choice, with coffee pot in hand, re-filled my cup and left.

"I'm so glad I didn't have to drive over that damn bridge to see you." I smiled, then took a long sip from my coffee cup.

Mitch's eyes sparkled. "It was great timing! My showing being right near your house? What are the chances? I love second showings because the clients are serious about buying. The only bummer is my manager always shows up and makes me nervous."

He exuded endless confidence, and it was surprising anyone or anything could rattle him. Except maybe his favorite director, Martin Scorsese. The time he'd been fired for smoking on the set of a Scorsese film, he'd badgered himself for weeks. "I should've known better," he repeated over and over. My attempts at comforting him were to no avail. "How could I have been so stupid? Not knowing the specific rule about his smoking ban?" He'd been upset for weeks after, but the silver lining was that he never smoked again.

"She makes you nervous. Why?"

"She's hot, and wears these tight-fitting shirts, without a bra. I hate to admit this, but I have a crush on her and it's hard concentrating when she's around."

He had a crush on her. Wait, what? "But you're gay." I blurted out as the waitress appeared with my sandwich and his soda. The rest of the conversation was tabled until she set the food down and left. "Are you straight now?" *Have you been sleeping with women? Have you had girlfriends? If so how come you weren't interested in me?*

"No," he laughed. "I'm just not totally cold to women." So casual and off-hand, like he was telling me about a new pair of jeans he'd bought while my stare of disbelief spoke volumes. "It's really *not* a big deal, Rose." Mitch reached across the table and took half of my sandwich. After a hefty bite he returned it to my plate. "I gotta pee." He sprang up. "Better not let me catch you near that cigarette machine." He headed towards the men's room and left me and my very confused thoughts alone.

"It's not a big deal." What do you mean not a big deal? Maybe not for him but for me it was huge. My mind raced back to NYC during our acting days together. Vivid memories about The White Horse, a bar in Greenwich Village, played inside my head. We went there every Tuesday night, regulars, after Stephen's acting class ended. Seated across from each other and sipping cheap white wine while we dished about everyone in class. AIDS, touted as the new gay

disease, was all over the news. Gay men were stigmatized, and many never came out of, or retreated further into, their closets. But not Mitch. "People need to stand up," he'd said and was disgusted by his friends who remained silent and allowed gay shaming by the media. He went off on a diatribe about his sexuality and recounted how he loved men. "I'm proud to be gay!" He declared. That night, I pried my head out of the sand and stopped feeding my enormous crush with false hopes. With this epiphany came zero hope we'd ever get together and that we would remain in the friend zone forever.

"Aren't ya gonna eat your sandwich?" He'd returned from the bathroom and slid beside me. "Hey. You okay? Ya seem a bit out of it." Silence ensued, and a moment later he spoke. "You thinking about your mom?"

"Yes," I lied while his outstretched arm hugged me. The truth was, for the first time in months, thoughts about my mother, cancer, chemo, Heather, Dad, or anything else family related wasn't at the forefront of my mind. I'd recovered part of my old self, the part of me that was an artist and missed my life. The resentment of being yanked out of Manhattan and stuck in Florida bubbled below the surface of my mind and could no longer be contained. Despite being a native of the Sunshine State, I felt like I was a stranger in a strange, but all too annoyingly familiar, land. Reclaiming some semblance of my previous life gnawed at me. Thoughts of wanting this entire ordeal to end filled me with relief, guilt, and fear. How can I cope with the double-edged sword of not wanting my mother to die, but knowing that when she did, I'd be free.

My confusion continued long after my lunch with Mitch ended and added more guilt to my already full emotional plate. As mom's condition worsened, my fears escalated and the intensity of my guilt increased. Not a stranger to this useless emotion, I was determined not to let it dictate my actions. But determination and reality were two different things, and most days guilt won out.

The chemo left her weak, and walking became more and more challenging. She hobbled around the house and still refused the aid of a cane, walker, or wheelchair. Her hair had fallen out two months prior, yet the cancer wig remained untouched inside its box. "It's too hot to have that schmatta on my head. If my baldness bothers you, then don't look at me." She didn't mince words, and it was clear she'd cope with the side effects of her cancer treatment the way she dealt with everything else, in denial.

She agreed to wear a light cloth turban when we went out. Hindered by her immobility, those outings consisted only of doctor visits and chemo treatments. The nurses at the center continued superb care, support, and kindness. She no longer wanted French fries and was fast asleep within moments after her treatment began.

My visits to the cafeteria ended, and wandering the halls of the clinic was my new pastime. Walking towards the ladies' room, I noticed Dr. Herman, mom's oncologist, approaching me. "Rose, I was just coming to find you. Let's go into my office. We need to talk." *We need to talk.* Those four dreaded words halted my urge to pee. The grim reaper dressed in a white lab coat led the way into a small room at the end of the hallway.

Once inside his office, he shut the door while I sat down on a cold, leather chair. Seeing my mother's chart on top of his desk, my stomach twisted into knots. "We need to talk" never preceded good news. Ever.

Our chat was brief, and the news dismal. "It won't be long now," Dr. Herman said, as I burst into tears. He apologized for not having a tissue and suggested the ladies' room.

"But the nurse told me that the new chemo is helping."

"That was only after *you* insisted on continuing her treatment. She didn't have the heart to tell you it was a waste of time." He looked at his watch and seemed inpatient. "I'd told you that from the beginning." He refused eye contact as he picked up a waiting phone call. "The nurse shouldn't have gotten your hopes up," he concluded.

I bolted out of his office as if it was on fire, retreated inside the bathroom, and couldn't stop crying. Knowing I'd have to pull myself together before returning to the chemo room forced me to breathe. Several deep breaths helped a bit and I reached into my purse for some lipstick. Lipstick? Who was I kidding? No amount of makeup could conceal my pain. Especially my swollen eyes. Fumbling inside my handbag for sunglasses was my only recourse. Wearing the dark shades, I headed to get Mom. The walk seemed to take an eternity and consumed every ounce of courage I could muster.

Halfway to her chair, my legs refused to move. Glued to the floor, I stared at my mother's once animated, sparkling eyes, now glazed over with a distorted. faraway look. Her fragility jarred me. She'd been declining for weeks, but I'd refused to notice. But now it was evident, and I could no longer hide from the truth.

"What's wrong Rose?" Her razor-sharp tongue softened, and her words sounded faint and distant. In that moment I knew it was time to start letting my mom go. Time to stop blaming her for all my problems because she'd done the best she could. She loved me, and I needed to grow up and understand she was only human. Would I ever feel the same about Dad? "Take off your sunglasses, Rose. I can't see you."

My head tilted downward, and my eyes fixed on the white linoleum floor pretending not to hear her. "Rose, what's wrong?" She persisted.

I didn't want her to see me crying and shrugged my shoulders. My head felt like a thousand-pound weight as I straightened my neck and looked at her.

"What's wrong?" She repeated. How do you speak during an out of body experience? I was looking at myself through her eyes. One day I'd be *her* and my daughter would be looking at me. My non-existent child would be confused and grieving looking at me for answers and comfort. My body tightened as a significant shift pulsated from within. No longer my mother's little girl, I'd crossed over into full-fledged adulthood. My metamorphosis felt complete, and it was only a matter of hours until my mother was ready to cross over a different threshold.

"Want some French fries, Mom?" Sounding upbeat was impossible but French fries always made her smile.

"No, Rose. I want you to take off those glasses and look at me while I can *still* see you." Her words sounded garbled. I removed my glasses while I walked over to her treatment chair, then sat down beside her. She reached for my arm, and we sat hand in hand in silence. A silence that only a mother and daughter could understand.

Chapter 7

Out With a Bang

We said goodbye to the nurses. Knowing it would be the last visit to the treatment center filled me with profound sadness. Getting ready to leave, Mom couldn't catch her breath. An aid scrambled to find a nurse, who secured an oxygen mask over her mouth. Since the clinic had limited facilities, an ambulance was on its way to transport her elsewhere. An hour later we were inside an intensive care unit at Jackson Memorial Hospital. After several hours, and more than a few unanswered phone calls to Dad, I returned home to get a key that Mom insisted on having.

"It's in the bedroom, inside my nightstand," she'd repeated in muffled words. "Bring it to me," she'd pleaded.

Seeing Dad on the living room couch with Pirate Kitty perched on top of his lap was bizarre. "Is he okay?" I said to myself, unsure if I meant my cat or my dad. "Is the cat okay?" I said out loud this time, then set my car keys on the small wooden table near the front door and entered the room. It was an odd sight to behold. "Dad?"

"He's fine. I heard whimpering through your bedroom door and thought he might be lonely."

Thought he might be lonely? Dad, cat hater extraordinaire, was concerned about the feelings of a feline? Was he off his meds and dipping into mom's Ativan stash again?

"Dad, you okay?" I'd never seen him show any emotion other than anger and disapproval so, unless he was on drugs, this current scene made no sense. "Dad," I repeated, "what's wrong?" I sat down beside him as Pirate Kitty leapt off the couch and headed towards my bedroom.

His eyes welled up with tears and it was a while before he answered. But when he did, his voice shook. "It's your sister, Rose. We've lost her."

Feeling like I'd been punched in the stomach, I gasped, "Oh my God, Dad! Heather is dead?"

"No, Rose, she's not dead."

"Was she in an accident? Is she hurt?" Confusion persisted while Dad buried his head into his hands.

"No," he whispered, and then heaved a large sob, followed by another. His gut-wrenching outpour of grief continued numbing me into an uncomfortable silence. *She's not dead. But the man of steel was crumbling, so something horrific must've happened.* Staring at the wallpaper peeling off the wall on the far end of the living room, my head pounded while trying to clear my mind. *C'mon Dad, what the fuck happened?* But asking more questions before he was ready to answer would've been futile. Dad couldn't be pushed for information.

"He only talks when he wants to," mom told us at an early age. Dad's lack of communication wasn't because he didn't love us. "He loves you very much," she'd assure us. But his love was conditional and dispensed on his terms and timetable.

After fifteen minutes, Dad's sobs concluded. "She's joined a cult, so she might as well be dead. A goddam cult." He blew his nose into the sleeve of his shirt, and I bolted off the couch in search of tissues. *A cult? Heather?*

Unable to find tissues, I grabbed a handful of napkins off the kitchen counter. "How do you know?" He reached out for the napkins while I sat down beside him. *Had he dreamt this during his afternoon nap and thought it real? Or was he more out of touch with reality than usual?* "Dad, how do you know this?" I repeated.

"She called! I know what I heard on the phone." His tone was belligerent. "I know what I heard!" he snapped. Silent and bewildered, while listening to him explain Heather's new lifestyle, my head continued throbbing. She was living in Sedona with the stranger she'd met at a bar. They'd made a home inside a yurt by the side of a mountain while waiting for some spaceship to pick them up and take them to another planet? The more he elaborated, the more I suspected he'd had a psychotic break. My sister would never live in a tent, not even a fancy one like a yurt. And she was scared to death of flying. Unless the UFO was giving away tremendous amounts of tax-free cash, there was little chance any of this info was reality.

"Don't tell Mom," I pleaded. She didn't need to hear this, not now.

"Where's your mother?" His eyes widened.

"Dad." The words fumbled inside my mouth. "The doctor admitted her to the hospital because she couldn't catch her breath after her treatment."

Dad bowed his head and his sobs returned. "She's my best friend!" And with a rare vulnerability, he asked if she was going to die.

Where had my Dad been all these months? Reminding him of how ill Mom was, and suggesting he come back to the hospital with me was useless. "Don't you want to say goodbye to her?"

"No." Dad shook his head, then reiterated how he couldn't go to hospitals because he didn't want to catch anything. "I wish I could go, but I can't."

Bewilderment morphed into disgust as I raced into my parents' bedroom. How could my Dad *not* go back to the hospital with me? Wasn't supporting family something *normal parents* do without question? Then I remembered that my father was hardly normal. A moment later, while digging through Mom's cluttered nightstand, I spied the small key on a silver chain hidden underneath some tissues. Was this the key to the Holy Grail? Would it open the door to a hidden room where all the family secrets were stored? Perhaps it opened a treasure chest, a locked box with piles of unreported cash inside? Was this a key to a bomb shelter or was it just a key to nowhere? Clueless, with key in hand, I raced back through the living room, grabbed my car keys, and left.

Half an hour later, back at the hospital, I walked down an empty corridor covered with red, white, and blue crepe paper. The decorations made no sense 'til I spied several balloons and a banner in front of the nurse's station. "Happy 4th of July," the streamers read in big black letters. Consumed with caring for Mom, I'd forgotten what day it was, let alone the month.

The sole nurse overseeing the nurse's station was on the telephone. "Excuse me." My tone of voice was polite, but she didn't look up and continued her conversation. After several minutes of being ignored, sweat poured down my face. *Was I invisible?* My patience was growing thin and a few minutes later I tried again, but this time my attitude was far from gracious. "Hello!" She still didn't look at me but acknowledged my presence by raising her hand. I didn't know sign language, but it was clear she wanted me to stop interrupting her.

"Are you Rose?" A voice from behind me asked and I turned around and faced her. "I'm Florence, the intensive care nurse. Are you Rose?"

"Yes, I'm Rose."

"Your mom keeps asking for you." She pointed to a hospital room across the hallway. "Keep your visit short because she's in tremendous pain," she said casually, as if it was the fiftieth time she had said it today.

Of course she's in pain! "Give her something!" My voice escalated, and its intensity was downright out of character. Now channeling Shirley MacLaine from *Terms of Endearment*, I demanded more drugs.

"I'm on it." The nurse seemed unfazed. Perhaps she'd been in this scenario before and was immune to emotional outbursts. "Is there someone I can call? You shouldn't be alone." Her eyes were soft and caring as guilt washed over me for berating her.

I bowed my head and fought back tears. "No." She inched towards me and attempted a comforting hug, but the last thing I wanted was sympathy from a stranger. Florence Nightingale might've meant well but her kind gesture made me feel even more alone. The people that should've been here weren't. Filled with white hot anger, I turned my back to her and walked away.

My feet felt leaden as I walked across the hall and opened the door to mom's room. The first thing she said was she needed a cigarette. "No Mom, not now. The nurse is getting you something to make you feel better."

Mom's feisty nature returned. "Did you bring the key?"

Ooh, the key. "Yes. What's it for, and why do you want it?

"To give to *you*."

"But what's it for?" I repeated.

"It's to a safety deposit box at--" she began but her coughing persisted. "There's a letter in my nightstand explaining everything." She gasped for breath while my eyes searched the room for the nurse's call button. "Don't call that nurse." She'd regained her composure and started insisting on a cigarette. "I'm begging you, Rose."

It was soul crushing not granting her this dying wish, but she was in an oxygen tent and smoking around oxygen wasn't a good idea. (Or so I heard? But I wasn't a doctor.) After crossing the room and climbing onto her bed, her breathing seemed better. Nestled beside her, the pain coursing through her body seemed to abate. But a moment later it returned tenfold, and her body trembled beside me. "Just give me a goddamn cigarette and go home!" She moaned. She didn't want me to see her like this. I ignored her pleas while stroking her forehead, and her quivering stopped. Her eyes closed and then my eyes shut as well. Resting my head upon her chest, sounds of her labored breathing filled the silence.

I was eight years old again and back inside my childhood bedroom. She was out of breath from running all the way back from our neighbor's house down the block.

"Rose, tell me *everything* that happened with that boy." Her eyes pierced me. Too ashamed and guilt ridden, I'd omitted important facts. Telling her a naked boy forced himself on top of me and ejaculated on my bare chest was impossible. I didn't even know what had happened, except that the experience was frightening and made me feel dirty and ashamed. The assault was so terrifying that I'd blocked it out and buried it deep inside my subconscious. She'd accepted my Disney-esque, sanitized version of the story and didn't push. But she knew there was much more than what was presented. She'd held me so tightly that day, breathing was almost impossible. "I'm always here my Rosala," she reassured me. "If you remember anything else, you can tell me. I promise I'll always love you." But I never revealed the truth, and stuck to my story and, over time, I believed it too.

Mom's coughing snapped me back to reality.

"I'm choking here, Rose." Her speech sounded muffled. "Please, I need a sucking candy."

My hands shook while emptying the contents of my purse onto her bed. I plowed through the accumulated crap, determined to find something, but found nothing.

"Find a vending machine," Mom instructed in a hoarse whisper. "Get mints, anything, my mouth is so dry." A mint? A MINT?

Another morphine drip was what mom needed. And, at this point, so did I. *Where the hell was that nurse?*

My purse and its belongings were left strewn on top of the bed while I raced out of the room. Panic-filled eyes searched up and down the empty corridor of the eighth floor, but to no avail. While I headed to another floor, I realized I'd left my purse behind. My head throbbed, and the walls of the corridor were closing in. My legs moved in slow motion while some deep breathing staved off a panic attack. Even if I located the vending machine, without money with me, buying the Lifesavers would be impossible.

Perhaps they had something at the nurse's station. *Where the hell was that friggin' nurse with those drugs?* A few minutes later, after I regained composure, a nurse's station appeared a few feet in front of me. *Do you have any complimentary mints?* I'd ask the nurse at the desk. However, my request was preempted by a very loud noise sounding like an explosion.

"These fireworks keep getting earlier and earlier ever year," an orderly wearing green scrubs and toting a mop and pail, laughed. Then a fire alarm sounded and moments later all the medical staff appeared. *Where had they all been hiding?* A sea of green and white swirled past me, rushing towards my mother's room. Leaving the nurse's station and following them, a minute later I was confronted with billowing black smoke that came from the corner where Mom's bed was.

Mom had found my emergency stash of smokes and fulfilled her final wish by having a last cigarette--on Earth, that is.

"Wake up, wake up." Someone was slapping my face as my eyes opened then stared at the strange surroundings.

Where am I and who are these people? My mouth moved, but forming words was difficult. "Where?" Was all I could manage.

"You're in a hospital." The nurse's eyes met mine as she nodded her head.

"In a hospital?" More confusion followed. "Am I sick?" Vague recollections of the past fifteen minutes echoed inside my head.

The nurse sensed my bewilderment and explained about the chaotic scene at hand. The police and firemen rushing about like there'd been an explosion. Which of course there was. "Your mother's bed exploded. And you fainted." *How could I have slept through all that?* She smiled warmly then helped me to my feet. A moment later we were inside a small office. She shut the door behind her then offered up some orange juice as the door reopened and the head nurse entered.

"*There* you are. We need to go over these." She waved some papers in my direction.

"She just lost her mother," Nurse Orange Juice said. Although still dazed and disoriented, I was grateful that nurse O. J. spoke up on my behalf.

With pursed lips, the other nurse enlightened me that the explosion probably wasn't covered by insurance and would have to be dealt with. "Your family may be responsible for thousands of dollars in damages." She was indeed the bearer of bad news.

"This matter can be handled another time." Nurse Orange Juice gave nurse Pursed Lips a stern look then escorted her out of the office. The two women lingered in the hallway and jabbered away. The office walls were thin and overhearing their conversation gave way to terror.

Recovered from the fainting spell, now panicky thoughts about money set in. My family didn't have endless resources for a hefty hospital bill! *What if we can't pay and are arrested, and must serve jailtime?*

A few minutes, later my fears were shared with Nurse O. J.

"It's highly unlikely that will happen. There are ways to get around this."

"There are?"

"There wasn't a video camera taping your mother. Where's the proof?" She smiled and offered up another juice box.

"I need to tell my mother!" Bolting up out of the chair, but Nurse Orange Juice grabbed my shoulder.

"Your mother has passed." Her eyes were gentle and voice kind while she sat me back down and offered to call someone. But there was no one, except for Mitch. *If only I could remember his phone number!* The reality of my mother's demise hadn't quite sunk in.

"Is there someone I can call?" She repeated.

Shaking my head and slumped in the chair, I was unable to move. Hours passed and it was almost one a.m. before I was functioning well enough to drive home.

The enormity of the tasks at hand bombarded me during the ride home. People needed to be contacted and informed. But it was the wee hours of the morning, and I didn't want to be one of *those* callers. Besides, except for our family and a few close friends, no one else knew the gravity of Mom's illness. "Don't tell anyone I have the "Big C," she'd instructed. And now it was up to me to tell them the truth and answer endless questions. These wouldn't be short, simple calls. Yes, the calls would have to wait.

Dad was seated at the kitchen table folding a large pile of towels when I struggled through the door. It was a peculiar sight, (even for him) and especially at this hour. But nothing compared to the bizarreness of the previous several hours.

"I did all the laundry, so your Mother won't have to do it when she gets home." He continued folding the towels without looking at me.

There wasn't an easy way to let him know about her demise. "Mom's dead.," I blurted out while he continued folding.

"We're almost out of laundry detergent." He nodded towards the half empty box of Cheer. Denial? Psychotic break? Gas? Any one of those could explain his cold-hearted reaction to her death.

"Dad, did you hear me?"

"I heard you." He mumbled, as his body trembled. "I'm not deaf." A long silence ensued as he stretched an unfolded bath towel between his two arms, then lifted it up then draped it over his head. A moment later he used it as a king size tissue. "But life must go on," he wailed.

My feet moved toward him while he blew his nose into the newly laundered linen, but my mind was still at the hospital.

"She's gone. Is there anyone we can call?" The nurse had asked. I shook my head, and knew *I'd* be the one making all the phone calls. But not now. Going through her address book, contacting her small circle of friends seemed daunting. They'd be shocked and disbelieving. Anticipating their questions exhausted me and I was already at my exhaustion threshold. This task would have to wait.

"Mom's gone," I repeated as I embraced my father. His arms fell limp by his side as he continued weeping.

"She was my best friend," he muttered over and over. Then he stood upright, turned around and walked towards his bedroom. A moment later the quiet closing of his door was heard.

Pirate Kitty slept on top of me the entire night. We were both grieving, and he didn't leave for a moment. Racked with guilt, I replayed the events of the past hours and still questioned if my mother's death was all my fault. Those were *my* cigarettes, and *my* matches. If she hadn't found them…

"She would've passed an hour later. Maybe a day at most." Nurse O.J. reassured me. It wasn't as if Mom was in the hospital for a sprained ankle. But still, the nagging suspicion that it was all my fault prevailed. "You *do know* your mother was gravely ill?" She inquired. Yes of course I knew! Who did she think I was? My Dad?

Pirate Kitty planted on top of my stomach prevented a night of tossing and turning. The restlessness was contained physically but my mind raced. For a short while, my eyes closed but sleep remained elusive. Grief, coupled with relief, were my companions while staring at the ceiling. Then guilt once again reared its ugly head. How could I be *relieved* my mother passed? *Am I a monster for being glad the whole ordeal is over?* A voice from within reminded me that all the worry about test results, or how much longer we had together was no longer necessary. Also ended was second guessing my choices of medical care for her. Now there weren't any other options for another course of treatment. It was all concluded, and I'd done the best I could. (But had I?) This doubt nagged at my core and would haunt me for decades.

My long-awaited freedom had returned but I was held hostage by something else: fear. Intense fear! Yes, I was petrified. How was I gonna pick up the pieces of my life and move forward? "Breath my darling, nothing needs to be decided tonight," a faint voice whispered into my ear. Pirate was pushed to the side while I bolted upright and looked around, but no one was there. The early morning sunlight filled the room, and these issues, like the phone calls, would have to wait. Life had a way of working out. (Didn't it?) It had been a long ordeal and now my Mother was at peace, and as much as I hated to admit it, so was I.

Chapter 8

Heather

A handful of mourners huddled together beneath a canopy ten feet away from her gravesite. Storm clouds threatened and lightning lit up the dark skies while a rabbi spoke. Shocked and exhausted, my brain had shut down and my ability to comprehend what was going on around me was nil. Mom's funeral was a blur of prayers, songs, and people with solemn faces all dressed in black. Everyone except for Heather, who wore an all-white ensemble. Just like Dad predicted, she'd shown up to the funeral and stood towards the back as the service continued. She'd smelled money all the way from Arizona and wasn't going to pass up claiming her inheritance.

When the rabbi's words concluded, Mom's plain pinewood casket was lowered into the ground. A few moments later, a heavy shovel was passed around for the mourners to heave dirt on top of the coffin. This was a Jewish tradition of showing respect and everyone participated except for Heather.

Dad was the last partaker and found himself challenged by the weight of the earth held on top the shovel. Or perhaps it was the weight of the day that had stalled him over her gravesite. The rabbi saw him struggling and ran to his side to help. Afterwards Dad turned to me, eyes shining, "I'll be there soon." He nodded towards the gravesite and sounded upbeat. "Right next to your mother." His inappropriate comment didn't faze me. Nothing did.

It was a small plot of land he'd purchased as her Mother's Day gift several years prior. It was located near a bench and underneath an old ficus tree that reminded me of the one near our house. "She's gonna love it here," Dad remarked as we walked away from the gravesite and out of the cemetery.

Heather walked between Dad and me. Not only did she smell money; she smelled. Bad. Really bad. Didn't they have showers at her cult site? Was body odor a sign of cult respect? A few minutes later, my sister upped her pace and strutted a few steps ahead of us. Her scent was atrocious and walking downwind from her was nauseating. We were steps away from the car as thunder roared and the skies opened. A downpour ensued. Drenched, we climbed into the backseat of the waiting ride. Dad sat next to the driver and started complaining. "Such a waste of money, when I could've driven us." He was disgruntled about the transportation costs and spewed out his resentment the entire trip home. Did he think we were gonna rent a U-Haul, hitch it to the back of the Dodge Dart, then dump Mom's coffin inside?

Heather's transformation was bizarre. She'd never been a conformist. No one would have guessed that she could, and in fact did, join a cult. As kids, Mom begged her to join Brownies, The Girl Scouts, Campfire Girls, or the 4-H Club. "Just give it a try!" Mom pleaded, desperate to get her to socialize, but Heather was a loner.

"Those club uniforms are disgusting," she'd respond. But Mom persisted (nagged) while Heather dug in her heels. "I hate all the girls in those clubs." She'd bark at our mother until mom had no choice but to back off.

Dad encouraged Heather's antisocial behavior. "They're all a bunch of schleppers." (Schleppers is a Yiddish word for lowlifes.) She was always Daddy's little girl. They were like two peas in a very unappetizing, odd pod.

Decades later, the nonconformists sat beside me, clad all in white. Prior to this moment, she'd never worn white, claiming it made her look fat. But now, here she was, draped in it with zero personal hygiene to boot. How was she going to get the smell out of her cult attire? Obviously, only I grasped the irony of the situation because Heather ranted about our parents' foul odors during her teen years. "Baby powder is ineffective. You need deodorant." She got in their faces without an ounce of subtlety. "You stink," she'd told them daily. I bowed my head and continued holding my breath, listening to Dad's complaints until we arrived home.

Once inside, Dad headed to the refrigerator and removed a premade cheese sandwich from the second shelf. Tonight, we'd be spared the danger of a fire as he skipped his ritual of heating his Dagwood cheese sandwich in the toaster oven. With wooden toothpicks still stabbed through the tower of bread and cheese, cold dinner in tow, he put on his slippers and shuffled off towards his bedroom. I ordered a pizza, then sat at the opposite end of the lime green Formica kitchen counter and half listened while Heather elaborated about her new lifestyle. She confirmed that she was living in a tent and sleeping in a sleeping bag. She was now a vegetarian and gave up her daily doses of Tab. Dad's accounts were correct. However, he'd said nary a word about her change in personal hygiene.

Her demeanor was different as well. Once chaotic and confrontational, she was now calm and collected and seemed at peace. "I'm happy," she said. Happy? Those two words had never been uttered by my sister. But she seemed very content. When was the other shoe going to drop? Cult life evidently had a stabilizing effect on my sister. And so did Kevin, her newfound love. Kevin must've loved her very much. It would take a shit ton of adoration to endure her smell.

"Deodorant, mouthwash, toothpaste, they all contain carcinogenic materials," she said, as if reading my mind. No surprise she'd stopped using hygiene products, but I questioned her rationale. Before we were able to debate this theory, she moved onto another topic. "I won't be allowed on the spaceship if I have a preexisting condition. All those chemicals cause cancer, Rose!"

Spaceship? She droned on about intergalactic travel and seemed annoyed when I mentioned more earthly matters.

"Of course I brush my teeth!" She was indignant. "But I use *organic* toothpaste and rinse with filtered water." She rolled her eyes and shook her head in that condescending, judgmental way that was so familiar. The old Heather was back, and I felt foolish thinking she'd changed.

"The world is ending soon, and the mothership is coming to save all believers," she spouted. All doom and gloom! Strangely comforting, some things never change.

"How?" As soon as the question slipped out, I regretted it.

"By transporting us to the distant planet of Klaatu Klaat." Was that near the planet Mars? The pizza delivery guy was at our door, and I was saved by the bell. Maybe I should ask the pimpled seventeen-year-old where Klaatu Klaat was located or whether aliens lacked noses to better tolerate human body odor?

But the pizza's arrival didn't deter her. More details about the alien spacecraft transport continued while I picked at my slice. With her new purist attitudes and behavior, it was amazing she'd agreed to eat a vegetarian pizza. She stuffed her face with the forbidden food, (except the Brussels sprouts, which were meticulously picked off and placed on the counter) pausing only to drink Tab (the devil's juice) between slices. She tried enlisting me into her cult and laid on a hard sell. My dinner settled like an iron anchor inside my stomach as the semi-spicy tomato sauce repeated on me. A little voice sounding like my mother was telling me to run. "I'm really tired and need to lie down," I said, exiting the kitchen and heading towards the den.

Heather trailed after me. "You only need to make a twenty-thousand-dollar donation to ensure getting a spot onboard the ship." And there it was! Her not-so-well disguised ask for money. After the den door closed in her face, she was still ranting. "You have the money! Now that Mom is gone." She screamed at the closed door while I settled onto the faux leather couch.

"Stop trying to scam your sister." Dad's voice echoed in the background.

She insisted she was only trying to save me. Dad said something unintelligible as I drifted off into a sound sleep.

The next day, a white, windowless van parked in our driveway.

"My ride is here," she announced and took a banana out of the fruit bowl before she approached me. "Good-bye, Rose." She grabbed my wrist then placed a wad of paper inside my hand. "In case you change your mind." She picked her white backpack off the floor and flung it over her right shoulder followed with a quick wave of her hand, and a loud slamming of the living room door. Sister dearest departed as quickly as an alien spacecraft on its way to Klaatu Klaat.

A few moments after she'd gone, I opened the crumpled paper.

It was a deposit slip for *The National Bank of Arizona* with "Beam Me Up" scrawled on the bottom left corner in my sister's handwriting.

I threw the paper in the trash, grabbed a Tab from the refrigerator and headed back to my haven, the den.

The week following Mom's funeral was difficult. We opted out of the traditional Shiva (a Jewish custom honoring the dead) but that didn't detour the garden variety of chaos following any traumatic event.

A few days later I found Mom's letter inside her nightstand's single drawer. It wasn't hard to miss, folded into a triangle and hidden underneath a half empty container of TUMS. The note was scrawled in her handwriting, filled with vague details about the secret safety deposit box that the key opened. Tempted to find out the details but unable to move, the idea was put on the back burner. "Don't tell your father or Heather," the note screamed in red capital letters. Although filled with curiosity, it would be unwise to drive to the bank. Drive? Hell, I couldn't even leave the house.

Heather's belligerent phone calls and badgering continued. "Rose, if *you* don't want to buy a seat on the spaceship, that's fine, but I need more cash." She greeted me on that late Sunday morning. Her absurd notions, outrageous request and ridiculous demands didn't intimidate me, thanks to Mom's Ativan

"They've upped the price for my ticket and since you *don't* want to go, I need half of your inheritance to secure my spot. It's what Mom would've wanted," she lamented.

Mom put several thousand dollars aside for both of us. Despite denial about her cancer, she'd left a will. Equal amounts to assure there'd be no fighting between us. My stomach clenched while listening to her laundry list all the reasons I *didn't need* money. "You're living rent free with Dad, and the world will be ending soon." Within moments, she'd upped her ask from half my inheritance to all of it. Forewarned by Daddy dearest about Heather's con man tactics, I was prepared and refused. "You're so selfish," she continued.

Sensing I wasn't going to cave, Heather played the guilt card. "Don't you even care about your sister? Just because *you* want to stay on this planet, and die, doesn't mean I do!" Then a slight pause before her grand finale. "It's always about you. You're such an attention whore. Always have been." Holding my breath, I knew her next tirade by heart. "Pretending to be raped when we were children. You've always wanted the spotlight."

Heather dressed in her cult garb was almost unrecognizable, however, the persistent attacks and greediness was all too familiar. Was this the universe's way of testing me, or would I be doomed to repeat our family history? Siblings turning on each other was our typical family pattern. Mom and her sister had screaming matches that made my ears bleed. Eventually they stopped speaking to each other. Dad's family were complete strangers. Despite his having several brothers and a sister, we'd never met any of his clan.

The reasons for our family's divide were due to money and unshared perspectives. Both Heather and I were young when these discourses occurred and we heard the hushed whispers. We couldn't fully understand the magnitude of destruction, but the result left us without aunts, uncles, or cousins.

"I want you two to love each other," Mom said repeatedly. She knew all too well the pitfalls that could lie ahead. "She's your only family," she whispered inside my ear. And at that moment, it was clear that liking my sister wasn't required, but loving her was necessary. It was up to me to break this chain of dysfunction that had plagued our family for generations.

Heather's ranting continued but something else had caught my attention. The smell of smoke. Bolting out of my bedroom and headed to the kitchen, I left the phone dangling while she babbled away.

Flames danced on top of the toaster oven, and I raced to the sink, filled up a water glass and put out the fire. Dad shuffled in just as the water hit the oven. "What the hell are you doing?" he barked. "You've ruined my lunch."

We'd been over this before, but he'd forgotten. (Or didn't care.) "The cellophane wrapped toothpicks holding your cheese sandwich together catch on fire, Dad! You need to remove them *before* placing it inside the toaster oven." He'd nodded, a sign that he'd understood, but here we were again as the toaster oven set fire to another triple-decker delight. My Dad, the cheese arsonist.

After the charred toothpicks and his toast tower were thrown into the trash, I remade his lunch. Granted, my simple sandwich didn't compare with his culinary creations, but firebugs can't be choosy.

Chapter 9

Den Days

The den still reeked from Mom's cigarettes and, in an odd way, the smell was comforting. The stale smoke was a subtle reminder that her spirit was always around. But Mom's rocking chair, where she'd spent hours watching television and complaining about Heather, Dad, my driving, my life choices, and my everything else was an excruciating memory and stowed inside the hall closet. The black, faux leather sofa was also a painful remembrance that remained. (I had to sit somewhere.) This den was *her retreat* only a few weeks prior, but now it was *my* fortress.

Six months had passed since I'd arrived home, and my anger and bitterness faded. Somewhere between her last hours in the hospital and the funeral, I'd let go of my resentment. She'd given me the gift of knowing her as a woman, and not just as my mother. Those days spent together allowed a glimpse into her humanness and strengthened a bond that would never be broken, not even in death. "A blessing in disguise." Her whisper rang inside my ear, as my eyes searched around, and half expected to see her. My heart then sank while reality hit; Mom was gone, and I was almost an orphan.

What now? My old mantra played on an endless loop inside my head. Returning to New York wasn't on my immediate radar. Hell, I couldn't even get off the couch. After months of feeling relevant and needed, now the complete opposite feelings prevailed. I had no purpose, so most days were spent lying on the couch, staring at the popcorn ceiling, and indulging in my private pity party. Oh yeah, and the Ativan. I was definitely indulging in the Ativan. Hours passed while conversations from past decades echoed in my head, but I couldn't remember yesterday or how my mom's laugh sounded.

During the '90s, instant access to memories wasn't available. It was years before advanced technology enabled pictures and videos to be readily accessible on your phone. All we had were faded photos that resided inside photograph albums or stored within treasure boxes.

What I wouldn't give for one more conversation. This time I'd pay close attention to the detailed stories repeated a hundred times over. Part of me yearned for her unfiltered opinions and suffocating hugs. Her obsessing about the should'ves, could'ves, and would'ves, wasn't healthy. She'd spent a lifetime filled with regrets and now I was repeating this pattern. Something had to change before I turned into her, but stuck in a lackluster haze, functioning beyond the bare minimum, was impossible. My caretaker role was replaced by that of a catatonic mess stretched out on the couch. Perhaps this was a normal part of the grieving process, or maybe I'd taken too much of her leftover Ativan.

What now? I repeated over and over but couldn't find an answer. I wanted to go back north and continue my previous life. Pick up where I'd left off, if only my body could get off this couch. I'd return someday, but first I would have to actually stand up. *Am I having the nervous breakdown my mother talked about?* Perhaps it was premature to think about going anywhere. *Good thinking.* I patted myself on the back, took another Ativan, then drifted off to sleep.

Loud knocking startled me awake. *Where am I?* I bolted upright and felt disoriented. The knocking continued and then I heard Mitch's reassuring voice. "Rose, okay to come in?" *Mitch!* I got up and opened the door.

"I'm so sorry I couldn't be at the funeral." He engulfed me in his arms, and his tears felt wet upon my face.

"You were sick." I held onto him with a death grip. "I understand." He was the first glimmer of hope since Mom's passing and, for a moment, my mood lifted. He continued holding me as we walked back inside the den. A moment later, seated on the couch, he laid a white rose onto my lap with a small box of Godiva chocolates.

"You always know how to make me feel better." Now it was my turn to cry.

He handed me a tissue and continued apologizing. "I feel like such a bad friend. You needed me and I wasn't there." His eyes avoided mine.

"But you had a contagious virus and a fever of 103." I shook my head then a moment later, a faint smile crossed my face. "We know how my Dad and Heather are."

"Yeah, pretty obsessive germaphobes." We both laughed as Mitch's guilt abated and his laugh morphed into near hysteria. "Your dad answered the door holding a handkerchief over his face." The laugh fest continued. For the first time in days, being alive felt okay. "And he had on latex gloves." Mitch was on a roll. We howled as Mitch edged closer then put his arm around me. The feel of his warmth soothed my anxiety, and I rested my head on his familiar shoulder as my shrieks of laughter became wails of tears. Remaining silent as he stroked my hair, we sat together for a long while. He dried my face and then put his head on top of mine as we feel fast asleep.

Dazed and confused, I jolted out of a sound snooze. The pitch dark room lent no clue as to what time it was. Mitch was curled up in a fetal position at the far end of the couch and his soft snoring was uplifting. Ever since he'd mentioned he wasn't cold to women, I'd fantasized about sleeping with him. But my fantasy was more x-rated than the night we'd just spent together.

With eyes closed, I imagined the feel of his mouth on mine, as he gently stroked my neck. But what if I revealed my thoughts and he met my transparency with trepidation? Or even worse, rejection?

"I love you so much, you're the sister I never had." Chances were good he'd say *that*. And *that* had an all-too-familiar-ring. "You deserve someone better than me." Or, "but who would be my best friend then?" We were best friends, and jeopardizing our relationship was too risky. The mere thought of enduring any more loss was unfathomable. Perhaps we'd been together in another lifetime and that explained our magnetic pull. My soul knew he was my twin flame, but in our current incarnation anything other than friendship was a bad idea. Besides, we were too much alike and craved conflict and drama to get our fires burning. We were two pieces of white bread with peanut butter inside when champagne and caviar were needed to create passion. Our friendship was perfect the way it was. It was enough. (It needed to be enough.) Thoughts about anything more with my best friend were put out of my head and the fantasizing halted. (At least for now.)

Sitting on the couch listening to the sound of his snoring was reassuring as my thoughts about a physical relationship drifted away. We shared a rare emotional intimacy that most people failed to experience.

"If it ain't broke, don't fix it." My mother's voice whispered inside my ear as gratitude filled my heart celebrating our unique connection.

A few minutes later Mitch awoke, sat up and rubbed the sleep from his eyes. "Good morning my Rosala." *Rosala*! *Rosala*! No one ever called me by that name except for mom.

"If it ain't broke, don't fix it!" Mom's voice echoed.

"How ya feeling?" Mitch asked. A smile crossed my face as we looked at each other. I leaned over and gently kissed his cheek, and for the first time in months, I felt okay. It was indeed a good morning.

Chapter 10

Short Trip to the Bank.

Hidden within my fortress, sprawled out on the sofa while staring up at the ceiling was getting old. Fear of getting couch sores motivated action, so I curled up into a fetal position. My repositioning didn't minimize the deep-seated feelings of disappointment and failure. No longer able to ignore the gut belief I'd let Mom down prompted a burning desire to honor her. It was time to take action and do something to assure her I'd paid attention to her decades of endless hocking. Now was the time to move forward. I got my fat ass off the couch and into a long overdue shower.

"See what's inside the safety deposit box." A little voice trailed behind me. I turned around, expecting to see her, but didn't. My stomach clenched while envisioning the short jaunt to the bank.

Is it too soon to leave my fortress for a test drive? Am I stable enough to develop a real plan of action? Can I remember where I left the car keys?

"Get in the goddamn car," the voice whispered.

It was the first time back inside the old jalopy without Mom. The engine started while a wave of sadness surrounded me. I felt unsteady. *How will I manage the drive without her backseat driving? Would I hit the brakes without mom's hand hitting the dashboard?*

Ten minutes later, the century-old white bank situated in the middle of a long Miracle Mile block appeared. After walking through the giant glass doors, a bank officer pointed me in the direction of the safety deposit boxes.

A moment later, a security guard opened the door to the large vault and followed me as I stepped inside. Sequestered within the sterile room felt like being inside a miniature mausoleum. Countless cubicles resembling post office boxes lined the walls. Finding the correct box holding Mom's stainless-steel case was a daunting task, but the bank official was more than happy to help. After a brief search, the safety deposit box was located and the bank official and I both inserted our keys. "Thank you." I watched him leave the vault as a wave of dizziness ensued after removing the long metal container out of the wall. Then, seated on the bare floor with legs crossed, my clammy hands removed two envelopes from the box. One was yellowed with age and sealed with a government emblem. The other envelope, a deep shade of red, had my name scrawled on it in my mother's handwriting. Taking a deep breath, the red envelope was opened first.

"My darling Rose. If you're reading this letter, that means I am no longer on this planet. Yes, put a fork in me cause I'm done. You were my rock and the only thing I lived for. I can only imagine how lost you feel without me. I'm filled with sadness that you don't have anyone watching your back. Your self-serving and clueless dad and sister can't be counted on, and it would be best for you not to expect anything from them. Especially emotional support. It is for *this* reason I'm informing you about the baby I had in 1946 then gave up for adoption. He was a little boy, born out of wedlock, who I only got to hold for a few moments before the nurses barged in and took him away."

Mom had a baby out of wedlock? I can't believe she hid this from me. What else don't I know about my mom?

"Grief stricken, and sobbing for hours, I wanted to keep him. But barely eighteen and back then there weren't many choices for unwed mothers. My father reminded me how I was a disgrace to the family, and repeated daily we couldn't afford another mouth to feed. My mother dared not dispute him and spent many hours alone in her bed crying. I've thought about the tiny infant every day since."

Mom had sex?

"Ten years later, I met your father and after a short engagement we married and then, a year later, I gave birth to you.

I've never told him, or anyone except your grandparents about my ill-timed pregnancy. I loved the father, but he and I were in different worlds, and he wouldn't marry me. I wanted you to know about your half-brother as a reminder that you have family out there. Family that's part of me and will always connect us. Finding him could fill the void in your life I know you are feeling.

The other envelope contains a copy of sealed adoption papers to start the search. When you're ready. Or not. Do with all this what you wish. My hope for you is that you will never be lonely and find love. Please know I'll always be with you, my darling Rose. MOM."

Comprehending those words were challenging. *Mom was a teenager? Who had sex? I had a half-brother?* Putting a baby up for adoption was unimaginable, as mom was a bit of a hoarder and never gave anything away. Perhaps I really didn't know my mother at all?

Murphy's Law suggested that locating my half-brother would be like searching for a needle in a haystack. The mere thought of where to begin looking was unnerving. Ancestry.com wasn't yet a concept, nor was 23andMe. Seeking a child given up for adoption, so long ago, must be a long and costly process. Besides, didn't I have enough aggravation and suppressed anger from those relatives I actually knew about? I placed the idea of finding my long-lost brother on the back burner and tucked the two envelopes back inside the safety deposit box.

Decades later, this day would return to haunt me.

I drove home on autopilot, parked in the driveway, and sat inside the car for at least an hour. I knew the time to do something to honor her was now. But locating a lost half-brother didn't feel right. Trying to find him would surely be a wild goose chase down countless rabbit holes. And wouldn't the search be self-serving? It was not the time to be self-serving. It was the time to honor Mom, (wherever she was). Time to show her that her years of crossing boundaries and administrating well-meaning advice hadn't been in vain. Figuring out what to do was the problem.

Later, enveloped inside my second shower of the day, the warm pelting water cleared my mind so all the random thoughts and creative ideas could fill my brain back up. She'd always wanted me to go to law school. How hard could it be? I am pretty smart. The law school buildings at The University of Miami were directly across from the theater arts buildings where I'd spent four years of college. Was that a sign? And the school was located just up the street from my parents' home. Another sign? Hell, these weren't just signs, they were roadmaps.

A newfound sense of purpose filled me as I shampooed my hair. *But what if law school doesn't work out? Do I really want to be a lawyer?* "I know. If law school doesn't work out I'll get married." That's what mom would say, I told the can of Nair, and gave my legs a long overdue, razor-free shave.

For the first time in weeks, hope had finally found me. Envisioning a plan of action felt invigorating. Drying off with an oversized towel was soothing. One of my plans would come to fruition. Right? Now on a mission, Plan A installed a sense of purpose. I was feeling a lot more like my usual self. But plan B, getting married, was trickier. "One plan at a time," a faint voice whispered.

After my shower, the den's magnetic pull forced me back inside and onto the faux leather couch. Closing my eyes and taking a deep breath felt different. Yes, after ten days my hair was squeaky clean, but it felt like more than just cleared off dead skin cells. It felt like an epiphany.

Thoughts about plan B danced though my mind. *I'll marry the next person who takes an interest in me.* I bolted upright. *I'll stop looking for love and chemistry.* Ready to give up my fantasies, this revelation confirmed that it mattered not whom I married.

"There are no knights in shining armor," my mother's voice echoed.

My only great love had dangled bait on a string for a decade. I'd spent years chasing Ethan, only to face days and nights filled with disappointment and heartache all because I'd choose to ignore his straightforwardness. With Plan B, I'd heed warnings and bolt at the first red flag. Hell, I was done with marathons.

"Exclusivity and marriage aren't in my wheelhouse," he'd warned when we were in the friend zone. But the romantic inside me thought he'd change his mind and tuned out his repeated reminders. "I'm never getting married." He'd reassured me love had nothing to do with the kissing, cuddling, sex, and the intimate talks we shared. He made it clear that love had nothing to do with our relationship, at least not for him.

"You love the game-playing, not him," Mom offered.

Be it a game or true love, that chaotic mess taught me the valuable lesson of self-preservation. My heart and soul would remain safeguarded and never accessed by anyone else. Ever.

"What's love got to do with it?" My new mantra validated that getting married would be a cinch if plan B was needed. Newfound determination motivated me to get off the couch and into my bedroom. Pirate Kitty greeted me with a loud mew as I sat on my bedspread and combed out my tangled hair, still wet from my shower. He listened with rapt attention to details about both plans. Then there was plan C. How to locate my missing half-brother was an option but it was more like a passing thought because more pertinent and timely plans were on my plate.

"I have a plan C, sorta." Pirate Kitty rolled over on his back and shut his eye. "But I'll save that for another time."

A long-relieved meow signaled he'd heard enough, and our conversation was over.

Attaining an appointment with the University of Miami law school guidance counselor felt empowering. But as the date grew closer, a feeling of dread (or panic) grew. A week prior to the interview, my galvanized mindset diminished. Consumed with self-doubt and anxiety, bailing and aborting plan A felt like the best option. But I'd disappointed Mom so many times and didn't want to continue the pattern. *Mom would be so proud of me if I went to law school. Isn't making her proud of me the goal? I can do this.*

Chapter 11

Plans A and B

The week flew by and arriving at the campus parking lot, (forty-five minutes ahead of schedule) felt surreal. Thank goodness it was a coolish fall day with low humidity and temperatures barely over 80 degrees or I would have melted waiting inside the unairconditioned car.

Panicking while leaving the car, I sidestepped a large concrete stone. One misstep and a faceplant would've been inevitable. Filled with gratitude for my good fortune, I inhaled deeply and thanked the universe. Mom's face appeared, and her eyes smiled. "You've got this, Rosala."

A few minutes later, seated inside a small, empty office, sweat covered the back of my neck. *Breathe.* After three long breaths, Ms. Mezner, a gray haired, middle-aged woman wearing a tailored suit with a crisp white shirt entered. In black jeans and a paisley peasant top, one of us was dressed inappropriately. We exchanged salutations, (both wondering what the hell I was doing there), before she sat down behind the mahogany desk and scanned my file.

"You were a theater major?"

My claustrophobia kicked into high gear and the walls began to close in. Nodding my head as she looked through the file, I tried to shrink into the cushions of my chair. Disappearing into that chair would've been welcome. After a few endless minutes she looked up. "No math or science?" My face flushed. Did she think I was some slacker who wanted an easy ride through school? Math and science weren't required for my degree. I was a theatre major. I had a Bachelor of Fine Arts degree. Not just a regular Bachelor degree. My education was firmly based upon my deep-rooted passion for acting, not laziness or math.

"Yes."

"Yes, you have math and science credits?" She scanned the file again. "I'm not seeing that noted here."

"I meant, yes, no, I didn't take those courses."

She shook head. "That's going to be a problem." A steady decline of conversation then ensued as the meeting continued.

The forty-five minutes spent in that office seemed like an eternity. Walking back to the car felt laborious. After my dismal experience with Ms. Mezner Plan A was nixed. Her suggestion to take supplementary classes in math and science before applying to law school was just not going to happen. I already went to college and wanted a plan now.

One block before arriving home there was a faint whisper in my ear. "Plan B," the familiar voice said.

Discovering several newspaper ads and pamphlets for Jewish Introductions stuffed inside a kitchen drawer was the sign confirming Plan B was the right next step. The hair on my arms stood up as mom whispered, "When you're ready." She stroked my arm and the hairs flattened.

My stomach clenched while scanning the brochures. A match making service? The thought of using a middleman to find love made me uneasy. But this predecessor of JDate and Match was highly recommended. Countless testimonials on the back of the pamphlets claimed that marital bliss was right around the corner. The accolades praising the high caliber of people they met through this agency was encouraging. "Give it a try," mom whispered.

An hour later I contacted Jewish Introductions. After all, what did I have to lose except my dignity? The woman answered her phone on the first ring, "And how did you find out about our agency?"

A voice from above sent me. "From a brochure," I said.

In a robotic voice she explained the different levels of enrollment and their corresponding cost. However, today was my lucky day because they were promoting a fall special. "Buy one get one free," she suggested. Such a deal, two months of dates for the price of one. "You could be engaged by Thanksgiving," she prompted. My heightened hesitation seemed to add more urgency to her sales pitch. "Today only," she pushed.

And before you could say "Are you happy now Mom?" the woman with the mechanical voice had all my information entered it into their database.

After the second disappointing date, and more than ready to cancel, I found the phone number on the brochure and was determined to terminate my membership. Deal or no deal, this dating service was no bargain.

Mentioning all the drawbacks about the men they'd sent over encouraged Marge (the owner of Jewish Introductions) to lay on a hard sell and she pushed her agenda to the max. After twenty minutes, she'd convinced me to take one more chance. "I'll personally find that special someone for you," she assured.

An odd vibe emanated from Richard, who was cute in a Ted Bundy kind of way. He picked me up in a silver Corvette and we chatted while jazz music played in the background. I didn't pay much attention to where he was driving until we got to the secluded mangroves in Matheson Hammocks. This scenic area was part of Biscayne Bay, a place for kids to swim during the day, and a romantic spot where teenagers made out at night. However, I'd just met this serial rapist look-alike, and wasn't interested in a make-out session. It was dusk, and the empty parking lot gave cause for concern. After he suggested we get out of the car and take a walk along the dock, the sound of doors locking sent a shiver up my spine. The previous dates lacked excitement, however after this date, I'd be happy to escape with my life. "I don't feel well," I blurted. Sensing danger and growing more concerned when he didn't respond, all the blood drained from my face. He smirked and seemed to enjoy watching me panic. "Please take me home," I pleaded.

A moment later a car full of loud teenagers pulled up next to us. One of the kids tapped on the window. "Wanna join us for a beer," he mouthed.

Richard never opened the window. He turned on the car and backed out of the lot and sped away through the dirt roads leading out of the mangroves to the highway. We rode in silence until he reached my house.

"Night," he said as he unlocked the doors and I jumped out. My heart felt as if it was beating outside of my chest as he backed out of the driveway. A wave of relief followed as I stood in front of my house ready to barf.

"Why didn't you listen to your gut feelings, Rose?" The horror of that evening reminded me how important paying attention to gut feelings was. Something was off about Richard and the panic of being trapped in an unfamiliar place was all too familiar. I had been through this before. Suddenly, I was a teenager sneaking out of my house to be with Oliver. He was a British man in his early twenties who I met when he was working in the neighborhood, and I was out for a walk. Overly developed and looking much older than my fifteen years attracted predators like Oliver. He was mysterious and his accent engaging. I'd had a weird gut feeling he wasn't kosher either, but ignored it. As a rebellious teen, I knew Mom wouldn't have approved of Oliver, or his pet duck, and that gave me the incentive to carry on with him. Not wanting to hear her disapproval rendered me silent.

Our top-secret meetings consisted of walking his duck around the neighborhood, then stopping at 7-Eleven for a Slurpee. He was a maintenance man providing pool repairs and weekly care for several people on my block. Sometimes (when his clients regulars weren't home) I'd go with him and watch the duck swim in his clients' pools.

But one day Oliver wanted me to venture outside of the neighborhood. "Wanna run an errand with me?" He called from inside a white pick-up truck while I walked home from school. Knowing my mother would disapprove, I readily agreed.

A half hour later we were parked outside a dilapidated tenement in Coconut Grove. After securing Daisy the duck in the back of the truck, he retrieved a stack of books.

Recognizing the books bought a sense of security. "What are you going to do with all those encyclopedias?"

"We're going to sell 'em." Oliver saw my bewilderment and explained how we were going to pretend to be a married couple and knock on all the doors of the apartments hoping the residents would let us in and listen to his spiel. He was not only a pool maintenance man but also a door-to-door encyclopedia salesman. Oliver was ambitious.

"For some reason Americans are suspicious of opening their door to a single man, but with *you* by my side we shouldn't have any problem entering their flats." He flashed a toothy grin.

Mom had repeatedly told me never get into a car (or truck) with a stranger and now I understood why. My stomach tightened leaving his vehicle and my head pounded while my feet trailed behind him. At the first apartment, a young mother, with a small toddler hanging onto her left leg answered. "Can I help you?" She locked the screen door and seemed apprehensive. My fears intensified as she listened to Oliver's spiel while her eyes darted back and forth, then landed on me. "Thanks, but I'm not interested," she'd said midway through his presentation, then closed the door in our faces. My knees felt weak and anxiety washed over me. Something about this didn't feel right. As the sun started setting, and night was fast approaching, my worry accelerated into full panic. "I need to go home," I whimpered.

"Go home? We're just getting started." He wasn't pleased and his nasty tone of voice scared me. "Lazy Americans," he mumbled.

"Take me home," My voice piped up.

"But you said you'd help me, Rosie. Don't tell me you're going back on your word?"

"I feel sick." He didn't seem to give a rat's ass and tried to convince me otherwise. Feeling trapped, my demands to be taken home escalated and could be heard down the block.

"Will you shut up," he demanded. "You're a bit too old for temper tantrums."

Temper tantrums? My pleas were far from that level. Temper tantrums? I'd show him what *that* looked like. For fifteen minutes I amped up my screaming as a disgusted expression crossed his face. He shook his head as we returned to the truck. He took a flask of something out of the glove compartment and begin drinking while weaving in and out of traffic. Terrified he was going to have an accident, my eyes closed. "Cherry oh," he sang at the top of his lungs several minutes later. The truck wasn't even at a complete stop as I leapt out near the edge of my driveway. Even though Oliver and Daisy the duck were never seen again, the trauma remained.

Déjà vu. Feeling like teenage Rose was debilitating. Paralyzed behind a veil of shame and fear, as I curled up on the edge of the lawn and remained motionless until the moon was out of sight. *Why didn't I listen to my gut feelings? Will I ever learn? What will it take to find a normal, trustworthy guy?*

Chapter 12

A New Plan B

When Mitch first suggested his idea, I was skeptical. "But there's *already* a plan C."

"To find your long-lost half-brother? That's not a plan, that's a road to nowhere." He meant well, but sometimes my understanding friend was less than empathetic. "Sorry to be blunt, but I gotta be honest. When you told me about law school, I kept my mouth shut. Then your other plan, going out with random strange men. Do you know how worried I was about you?" He asked.

"Nothing happened."

"You could've ended up on a milk carton. Or worse!"

"I think that's only used to locate missing children."

"That's not the point." Sounding too much like my mother, he continued. "One of those weirdos could've murdered you." Mitch might've left showbiz, but still had a flair for the dramatic.

"Law school was the safer plan, and I'm sorry it didn't work out. If only you'd had those math credits." *Was he sighing?*

"And science," I whispered.

"Yeah, that too." He put his arm around me and kissed the side of my head. Instinctively he knew how emotionally debilitating the past months were and the importance of tender loving care.

"You could've met Mr. Right in law school, if you'd been accepted." Could've, would've, should've; the story of my mother's life. And now potentially mine too. *Was it genetic?*

"It would seem like now there's no chance of meeting a law student." He smirked.

"Seem?" The glint in his eyes was familiar. "What's going on?"

"My idea isn't a new plan; think of it as a new plan B."

"A new plan B?"

"A new and *improved* plan B. Instead of attending law school, or dating losers from that dating service, how 'bout a blind date with a law student?"

My face scrunched. "It's too soon." Barely recovered from the Matheson Hammock episode, feeling safe was my priority.

"This is different because Harold *isn't* a stranger, he's my friend." Had Mom inhabited Mitch's body and controlled his mind now? His words sounded pushy if not pushier than hers. After twenty minutes of hocking about Harold the law student, agreeing to think about it was a comfortable compromise.

Plan B, to marry just anybody to make Mom proud was aborted along with my membership to Jewish Introductions. Perhaps meeting Mitch's friend would be okay. Maybe plan B two was actually plan B in disguise?

A week later, on a chilly day towards mid-October, the familiar mantra of *what next* played on an endless loop inside my mind.

As I slouched in a lounge chair in the backyard, a familiar whisper returned. *"Don't worry about it, Rosala."* Of course, Mom would suggest putting my head in the sand like an ostrich. But how could I not worry about it? Fixated on the dilapidated clothesline that should've been removed years ago felt like a metaphor for my life –

broken, useless, idle. My eyes closed but a moment later, the sound of footsteps approaching jolted them open.

"I'm glad you've traded in that couch for this lounge. Fresh air is good for you." He perched himself on the edge of the chair. "Harold really wants to meet you." Straightforward as usual, Mitch didn't waste a minute before mentioning his lawyer friend.

With several days to ponder his suggestion, my feelings were still ambivalent. Hell, clueless about everything, a blank stare was all I could muster.

"Rose," Dad's voice belted from the back porch. "You've got a phone call. Better come inside and take it. Maybe Broadway wants you back." *Dad cracked a joke. Am I on Planet Earth?* "Hurry, she's calling from New York." he barked.

New York? I bolted off the chair and headed into the house.

"Rose, it's Julie from *Star Finders.*" The rumors were wrong and my agent whom I hadn't heard from for months, evidently *wasn't* dead. *Star Finders* was an ironic name, as her agency was a small boutique group who supplied background actors, under-fives, or day players to production companies filming in the tri-state area. There were no stars on their roster.

But how'd she find me here?

"Good thing your parents' phone number was listed on the emergency contact section of your profile," she said, as if reading my mind. A moment later she continued. "Remember the commercial you did last year? The one promoting Israel tourism?"

Recollecting my commercial repertoire was easy, as I'd only booked a few things. "Yes, we filmed at Newark airport."

"The casting director who cast that commercial contacted me about you…"

My heart raced with dread and anticipation. *Did she call to complain? Not satisfied with my job and wanted all my residual checks back? Had she found out I didn't have an updated passport? That made zero sense because we filmed in NJ. Why would I even need a passport? What if…*

"She's working on a feature film and requested you for a small part." *Wait, what? Someone requested me?* "Are ya interested?"

Was that a trick question? "Yes." My hand shook holding the receiver. *Somebody requested me? Inconceivable. After years of rejection, I was requested. Am I dreaming? Is this my big break? Is this my karmic reward for all the shitty times when no one was interested?* My mind raced back to the early days of my acting career. After casting me in a small role on the feature film *A Whisper of Opportunity,* the director decided he didn't like me. The experience of being fired, in front of an audience of crew members and other actors, was traumatizing. Humiliated and heartbroken, I was replaced while still on the set. Later, the truth unfolded about my replacement. She was the director's girlfriend-of-the-week, and he'd promised her a part. MY part. Although my career was just starting, thoughts of giving up showbiz were already crossing my mind. But instead of quitting, I'd had a pivotal awakening about how brutal the industry could be and decided to persevere.

"Are you available for a few days' work on a feature filming in Brooklyn next week?" She inhaled deeply on a cigarette.

Hell, my whole life was available! "Yes, I'm available." I tried keeping my enthusiasm dialed down, not wanting to appear overanxious.

"Your headshots are current?" She paused for a second. "You haven't had a nose job, have you?"

A nose job? I never even went to a regular doctor let alone a doctor with a knife! Was she kidding me? "Nope, same schnozzla."

"Great, you'll be playing an Orthodox Hassidic Jew." Back in the 90s her incredibly racist remark was commonplace. Jews were often characterized by the size of their noses. Julie was a nice person and didn't seem antisemitic. And even though I cringed hearing her words, I remained silent. Perhaps she was unaware that her comment was off-putting to members of my tribe. She didn't seem to realize that Orthodox and Hasidic were two different things either, and I wasn't about to correct her because I really wanted the job. Now wasn't the time to discuss religion. "Got a pen?" She waited as I grabbed a Flair from the junk drawer to jot down all the information.

"You okay, Rose?" Dad asked as I walked out of the kitchen nearly colliding in the doorway.

"I'm great!" The last several weeks, he'd made a miraculous recovery and didn't need me to babysit him anymore. He was self-sufficient and there hadn't been any toaster oven fires since he stopped using toothpicks to structurally support his cheese sandwiches.

"I'm beyond great! I'm going to New York!"

"Did someone die?" he asked.

I shook my head, and he shrugged his shoulders. Dad was back to his old uninterested-in-my-life self. If he needed something, he could always contact Heather, who was still in Arizona waiting for that spaceship. Although dealings with my sister ended shortly after Mom's funeral, I'd overheard Dad's weekly clandestine phone calls with her. She was Daddy's girl after all.

Mitch came inside the kitchen and my beaming smile spoke volumes. "Well?" he asked.

"My agent called, and I've got a few days' work on a film in Brooklyn." We jumped up and down like two eight-year-olds at a birthday party.

Delighted, but still determined to introduce me to his friend, he continued. "I hope you'll meet Harold before you go." His eyebrows arched as his intent blue eyes searched my face for an answer.

Knowing Mom would want me to meet this law student pushed me to agree. "Sure, I'm meet him." As soon as the words left my mouth, Mitch was halfway out the door.

"Great, I'll call him as soon as I get home. Talk to you later." His voice trailed off as the back door closed behind him and a smile of epic proportions crossed my face.

Our late-night phone chats were a huge part of my Florida lifestyle. We'd discuss movies and TV shows, then gossip about people we knew (or didn't or wanted to) from the City. Sometimes hours were spent schmoozing about nothing. But tonight's conversation was far from trivial. An important subject was on the table and not a moment was wasted on our usual banter.

"I hope you haven't changed your mind about meeting my friend." He sounded concerned.

"I'm a woman of my word," I reassured him.

Even though Harold lived with his mother, Mitch assured me he wasn't gay.

"Not that there's anything wrong with it," I chimed in.

He recounted Harold's situation more than twenty times, answering my repetitious questions in a calm, caring manner. "He's divorced and used to live in Europe. His ex-wife took him for everything and left him broke. He returned to the States and his mom is helping him out 'til he's finished with law school."

"So, he *lives* with his mother," I repeated.

"Yes."

"And he's *not* gay?"

"Oy, Rose, enough!" He'd lost his patience. *I couldn't blame him.* Then, for the first time during our long tete-a-tete, silence. But the quiet didn't last long. "Consider it part of your mission to make your mom proud of you."

He had a point. Meeting a nice man who wasn't a certifiable psycho would bring her heavenly peace. Her presence was felt as my eyes closed and saw her smiling.

"I'll meet him when I get back from NY." Focused on my trip back east, meeting someone right now was the last thing on my mind.

"No, meet him *before* you go." He listed all the reasons time was of the essence, and this introduction couldn't wait. "I'm telling Harold you'll meet him tomorrow evening," he concluded, and hung up the phone before I had a chance to say another word.

Chapter 13

Harold

The next evening the doorbell rang at precisely at six-thirty. I grabbed my handbag off the kitchen counter and walked to the front door.

"Hello." Stepping outside, I noticed his colossal mustache and oversized glasses. His beard hid the rest of his face. Mitch never mentioned anything about his friend's bird's nest. I'd never dated bearded men and had only seen facial hair this long and thick on rabbis. If this was the eighteen hundreds it might've been Abe Lincoln at my door holding a single red rose. *Maybe this guy is a Harley biker?*

"He can shave the beard and you can get him to buy new glasses," Mom's voice whispered.

"I'm so happy to meet you." He handed me the flower. "A rose for a Rose." A little corny but a charming gesture as no one had ever greeted me that way.

He opened the passenger's side door and once inside his small MG, Carly Simon's "Anticipation" blared from the radio. Part of me wondered if that was a sign, and the other part questioned if this was his mother's car.

"The only thing I got to keep from the divorce," he said, as if reading my mind.

The night air felt brisk as we drove with the top down. At a red light, Harold pulled a blanket from the back seat and handed it to me. "If you're cold? Or I could put the top up?"

Not waiting for an answer, he tucked the blanket around my shoulders. "Just in case." He smiled as the light changed and drove west as the sun was setting.

During dinner, I ate like a bird and smoked like a fiend. Glimpses of his beautiful hazel eyes smiled through his clumsy, unattractive glasses. His eyes told me he was different than other men from my past. Especially the ones from Jewish Introductions.

Midway through our meal, an unusual calmness was felt within. He was smart, charming, witty, and attentive. As we engaged in effortless conversation, I was still waiting for the other shoe to drop but, for the first time in months, laughing replaced loneliness.

With every sip of vodka, he became more appealing. The beard disappeared and as he got up to pay the check, his cute ass tucked into those tight jeans caught my attention.

Not ready for the evening to end, we went bowling at the local alley. The bowling Gods were with me as I scored three near-perfect games.

"Wow." His admiration seemed authentic and his masculinity unthreatened. Not many men would've been thrilled losing and his reaction indicated confidence. After closing down Bird Bowl we parked in front of my parents' house and talked.

"I hope to move out of Sara's place in a few weeks," he said.

"Your mother's place?"

"Yes, my mom's condo." It was odd he called his mother by her first name, and even stranger that my mother's first name was also Sara. On a whim, I asked him what her last name was.

"Goldman. Same as mine."

"No, her *maiden* name."

"Cohen."

"Your mother is Sara Cohen?" My jaw dropped.

"Yes. Do you know her?" He laughed.

"My mother's name was Sara Cohen too." The coincidence was uncanny. Both our moms having identical names was a sign. A big neon sign flashing in front of me.

"What are the chances of that?" He seemed to take the happenstance in stride and changed the subject. "What do you prefer, stage or film?" Someone enthralled hearing about my life as an actress felt flattering. Impressed with the ins and outs of showbiz, details about waitressing, coat checking, and temp jobs, (the in-between acting gigs) could wait. There wasn't a reason to tarnish his vision of me by mentioning *those* aspects of my career. Although excited for my upcoming film, he seemed uneasy about my return. "Promise me you'll come back from New York City."

The sun was starting to come up as he took both my hands in his and kissed them. He got out of the car and walked me to the door. "Goodnight, Rose."

It was an awkward moment before he gently brushed my cheek with his lips then stepped away. We both stood staring at each other knowing there was something magical and extraordinary happening.

Sliding my key inside the front door, a wave of sadness washed over me. Despite the early hour of the morning, I didn't want our date to end.

"It's just the beginning, " a quiet voice whispered.

Chapter 14

Harold or Manhattan?

Three days later I was Manhattan bound. Cotton candy-like clouds billowed outside the airplane window while I daydreamt about my several phone chats with Harold.

"Call me when you get there," he said.

As the plane reached its cruising altitude, excited anticipation about returning to the City replaced my usual angst about flying.

A few hours later, the Manhattan skyline appeared. Although my life had undergone a complete metamorphosis, New York City had remarkably remained intact during my absence.

Walking through the airport, my entire being felt changed as a newfound confidence emerged. My posture was erect, shoulders pulled back, and head held high. I was very different from the girl that had traveled through this same terminal several months prior. Perhaps losing my mother had helped me find myself. Perhaps realizing I couldn't rely on her anymore jolted me into adulthood. At thirty-five years old, it was about time.

Seeing the cabstand directed my attention elsewhere.

A few moments later, settled inside the taxi, a huge smile crossed my face. "Manhattan please," I told the driver.

The next day, sequestered within a holding area somewhere in Brooklyn, a production assistant presented the final specifics for the scene we were going to shoot. My head itched underneath the wig, and I was sweating beneath the floor length clothing. Portraying a Hassidic woman had its challenges.

"The bus parked out front will take you to the first location. A cemetery," the production assistant continued.

Cemetery? He blabbed away while I needed to pee. Certain there weren't toilets in the middle of a graveyard, I bolted to the bathroom.

Upon my return people, were boarding the bus and my pace quickened. A few moments later, the doors shut, and we were on our way.

The bus was packed. Seated among the actors were actual Hassidim to add movie magic to the film. Thirty men sporting long beards like Harold's and twenty-two women straight out of *Fiddler on the Roof*. Makeup and wardrobe did an outstanding job, as you couldn't tell who was real and who were Memorex.

My eyes shut and thoughts about my new romantic interest filled my head. "She's away filming on location," he'd boast to his law student buddies, all wondering who this new mystery girl was. The gig couldn't have come at a better time, giving credibility to who I was and where I'd been.

It was late fall, and a cold autumn wind was blowing hard enough to push the hair of my wig into my face. The cemetery was freezing and there I was, once again in a cemetery soon after my mother's passing. Rebounding from grief and watching the Hasidic men actors beat their chests felt surreal. The rabbi, sporting a waist length beard, recited Hebrew prayers in a loud voice echoing above the crowd. I shivered as more gusts of cold air bombarded me, and I was now glad wearing a sheitel was part of my costume. (According to Jewish laws, no one other than their spouses were allowed to see Hassidic women's hair and so all married females wore wigs, called sheitels, out in public.) No longer itching, the sheitel kept my head warm as we shot the same scene over and over.

Filled with sadness, this scene was incredibly reminiscent of Mom's funeral, a brief two months prior. It was art imitating life. The grief I felt was real. No acting here. An eerie chill swept through me, noticing all the bearded men.

Deep inside my soul, a mystical feeling was rising. *Was my blind date with the bearded man arranged from beyond? Had Mom sent me to this cemetery to assure I'd heed her message from the grave? After all, there are no coincidences.* (Were there?) Or was I just losing my mind?

A few hours later, we reboarded the bus and headed to the next location. The ride was quiet, except for the sounds of a few napping passengers snoring. Most of us were defrosting. As we pulled into a parking lot next to an old synagogue in Brooklyn, Mom's message became crystal clear. "I got your memo," I whispered to myself.

She was letting me know, with no uncertainty, that the amusing man wearing tight jeans with the cute ass was sent from her. "This is the one," she nagged.

While shooting the wedding scene, my epiphany was confirmed. Standing near the orthodox bride at an elaborate fake marriage ceremony that shot 'til dawn wasn't random. There was a reason for everything that was happening.

It was five a.m. when the bus pulled back into the original holding area. Night shoots were exhausting.

Although dog-tired, what the production assistant said caught my full attention. "Folks, there's a shuttle leaving in ten minutes from Woodbine Avenue for anyone going to Manhattan." *Woodbine!* Woodbine is a teeny tiny obscure town in the backwoods of rural New Jersey. It is also where my mother was born. It was another sign. My epiphany was confirmed.

Leaving from Woodbine Avenue aboard the packed bus, we headed back to the City. Like most, I drifted off to sleep as my mom, wearing her favorite tent-style housedress, gently patted my head. "Rosala," she said, as smoke billowed out of her mouth. "Harold is a mensch, (Yiddish word for a stand-up guy, a good person) so don't screw this one up."

"Okay, Mom." Stunned that she was allowed to smoke in heaven, I mumbled "I'll try not to" and drifted off.

Chapter 15

Debbie Downer and the Witch

The sound of four locks opening echoed throughout the hallway. Old wooden floors creaked as I tiptoed inside the apartment then eased the door shut. Staying at my residence wasn't an option because Flo's boyfriend had moved in, and that situation served my financial needs. When I'd mentioned my New York trip to Debbie she offered up her place. "Crash on my couch," she'd suggested.

It was seven a.m. but the middle of my friend's night. Her day started at noon because she was a struggling, stand-up comedian, who kept late hours while performing at comedy clubs throughout the City.

"Rose?" She called out from inside her bedroom.

"So sorry to wake you." Walking over to her doorway, a familiar sense of guilt consumed me while the back of my neck tensed. She had a way of making me feel bad about everything. Less than a minute inside her apartment and I was already apologizing again. Although she was a generous person, everything she did came with a price. How stupid of me forgetting that detail. When she'd offered up her couch during the film shoot, my gut feeling warned against it. *But it's only for a few days and I'll be away filming for most of it. And hotels are costly.*

"You didn't wake me. A phone call *for you* did," she said. I should've listened to my gut. Her words hung in the air for what felt like an eternity. "Harvey called about fifteen minutes ago. He wants you to call him back."

"Harold."

"Whatever." Her eyes rolled. Over the past three days, the few hours we spent together in between my film shoot were horrific. Constantly complaining about everything and trying to one-up anything I said, she had worn thin my good nature. And this last day was no exception. "It's none of my business, but how much do you know about this guy?" My stomach clenched while she spouted negative, unwanted thoughts regarding my whirlwind romance.

Part of me felt sorry for her. She'd always had a hard edge, but there was once a soft, vulnerable side that drew me to her. We'd spent hours hanging out when we waitressed together at The Rainbow Room. But now, a decade later, after two failed marriages and a string of trainwreck relationships, she was nastier then I'd remembered. Her weddings were beautiful, and I was a bridesmaid for both. "I think you're bad luck," she'd told me after her last marriage failed. At the time, I thought she was kidding, but in retrospect she was seriously blaming me for her failed nuptials. Now she viewed men, love, and life through an even more jaded lens then before. Time had taken a toll on her happiness and darkened her soul.

"How much do you know about this guy?" she repeated.

"We just met." Although it felt like I'd known him forever.

"Again, none of my business, but all these phone calls from someone you had just one date with seems a bit odd."

Part of me wanted to say, "You're right, it's none of your business." But she'd been burned and was just trying to protect me. Underneath her rough exterior was a good heart. (Wasn't there?)

She'd scoffed when the flowers came. "Sending you two dozen roses, after a date that didn't include sex or even a hand job, is just weird."

Her intentions were good. (Weren't they?) Or maybe she was envious and trying to rain on my parade.

I headed to the kitchen and tried ignoring her comments. Seeing the flowers that appeared a day after my arrival made me smile. "I hope I'm not allergic to them," she'd said, then sneezed.

Now each one had opened, and their fragrance was exhilarating. While I was adding more water into the half-full vase my stomach clenched again. *But what if she's right?*

Debbie got out of bed and brewed up some coffee. (There wasn't a crumb of food at her place. Besides the coffee, there was only milk and vodka.) We sat down at a tiny table inside her teeny kitchen as she continued her interrogation.

"Do you know anything about his past? He seems sorta..." She paused.

"Sorta what?"

"Stalkerish."

Stalkerish. She didn't bring a cloud to rain on my parade, she was bringing a tsunami.

"These flowers, the phone calls. It's a bit much. What happens if you don't like him after the next date, but he won't leave you alone?"

Someone not leaving me alone was never my problem. Ethan's non-committal behavior kept me hanging around for years. Hope sprang eternal as I waited for him to change his mind, but he never did! Was I the stalker?

"When a guy pays enormous amounts of attention to you right off the bat, sometimes he changes once you get to know him."

"That may be true, but--"

"Like Dr. Jekyll and Mr. Hyde." She took a deep breath and starred into my eyes. "You start falling for him, and once he knows he has you, he treats you like shit."

"But--"

"And he winds up being a controlling, narcissistic creep!"

She had a resting bitch face, even when smiling. Which was an odd paradox since her career was in comedy. After years of therapy, her self-proclaimed expertise at detecting toxic behavior seemed curious. If she was so knowledgeable about this, then why was she still attracting so many Mr. Wrongs? Maybe she was the problem. Not the men.

"You have to stay alert for the signs." She took a long sip of coffee and shook her head.

I'd seen the signs, but not the ones she'd mentioned. An overabundance of cryptic messages arrived loud and clear. Besides, mine were from a much more reliable source. The knot in my stomach eased and I relaxed.

I'm not a stalker and Harold isn't a creep. My mother would never send me someone like that.

"I just don't want you to get hurt," she concluded. A smiled cracked through her resting bitch face.

Harold has more to offer me than heartache.

"Time will tell," she said in a condescending tone. We finished our coffee. She put the two empty cups into the sink then headed to shower.

Her disposition had soured over the years. Back in our waitressing days there'd been hints of her negative and judgmental nature but now she'd bloomed into a full-blown intolerable bitch. "Good-bye," I said, shouting through her bathroom door. "Thanks for everything." Although my flight wasn't until late afternoon, I left Debbie Downer's dwelling as fast as my legs could carry me. With suitcase in hand and hours before my flight, I strolled along MacDougal Street. Mixed feelings emerged as a northwest wind whipped around the corner. My strong detached feelings magnified while I zipped up my coat. Thoughts about *where* I really belonged filled my head. The film shoot was fun, but something was missing. It lacked the thrill it once had. My burning desire to be an actress was gone and replaced by a less intense flicker of interest. *Should I fan this flame or explore other options? What do I want to do with my life?* The words were almost audible as the familiar mantra, *what next?* returned.

Suddenly in the middle of the block a familiar brownstone that had fallen into disrepair caught my attention. Peering inside the filthy floor-to-ceiling windows that adorned the front, I saw her. The windows might've been thick with grime, however there was no mistaking the woman clad in all black seated behind a large, freestanding card table. *The witch!* It had been several years, but she was still there, interpreting tarot cards and reading palms. Memories of my last visit to this clairvoyant emerged while I climbed the broken brick stairs to have my fortune told again.

"You will have a successful outcome no matter what you attempt," she'd said reading my palm all those years ago. A little vague, but her words bought me hope and that optimism was worth the ten bucks. A moment later, I stepped inside the small waiting room, which reeked of incense.

Not long afterwards, the witch ushered me into an adjoining room. Once I was seated on the wooden chair, my mother's voice whispered inside my ear, "Listen to her, Rosala. She knows."

The fortune teller squinted her small dark eyes as she studied my palm, then traced the lines with her index finger. A cold sweat ensued as she looked up. "You're looking for someone. Someone you've never met, who's related to you."

My half-brother, could she be talking about him?

"You should stop your search," she said.

"Why, is he dead?" Panic filled my voice.

"No, the person you're seeking isn't seeking you and won't be found for a while.

How long was a while? The vagueness of her comment made me question its validity. So many people thought fortune tellers were a joke. Was she just a conman taking advantage of a vulnerable person? Was I truly that naïve?

"You're wasting your time now." She redirected my attention to a long line at the base of my palm. "See? It's written here."

"Oh." A confused smile crossed my face.

She pointed to another area of my hand. "Do the initials HG mean anything to you?"

Harold Goldman! Oh my god, his initials were carved into my hand!

She took both my hands in hers and bowed her head. "There was a lot of pain, struggle, chaos, and confusion in your life, but I see clarity ahead. Stay focused on what is happening in the present." She looked up after a moment. "For another twenty, I'll read your tarot cards?"

What if the tarot cards predict something bad?

"Stop while you're ahead," Mom's voice whispered.

Not wanting to press my luck, and running low on funds, I declined her offer and schlepped my suitcase down the rickety stairs. Still stunned by this latest sign, I wandered down MacDougal. The sounds of little children singing "Itsy-Bitsy Spider" was somewhere off in the distance. A moment later the group of children was right behind me, and I sidestepped to let them pass. There was a tall woman who kept them in tow as they continued walking and singing. School had let out. They appeared to be five or six years old. Perhaps they were headed home, herded by the tall lady dressed in plaid. They'd be greeted by their mother's embrace and enjoy an afternoon snack. Outfitted in matching uniforms, the children turned the corner the sight of which tugged at my heartstrings while the loud sound of my biological clock ticking drowned out their singing. Having children was never forefront in my mind, but after losing Mom, my maternal instincts ramped up. The urge had started shortly after turning thirty and been disregarded. But now, this desire was too strong to ignore.

Chapter 16

Finally Home

The City disappeared through the taxi cab's window and filled me with the same mixed emotions I'd experienced on MacDougal street. My whirlwind film shoot was exhilarating, but the multiple signs sent from the great beyond remained perplexing. Countless messages from Mom were noted but not altogether realized due to the chaos of showbiz. Now, heading back to Florida, I'd have time to unpack all the mysterious other-worldly communications along with my suitcase.

The driver was elated when I handed him my last two twenty-dollar bills and sped off to pick up another passenger. Would his next fare be another confused person trying to make sense out of their life or a young hopeful embarking on a NYC adventure for the first time? This fleeting thought ended as my left eye twitched entering the large LaGuardia airport terminal. A minute later, after scanning the arrival/departure boards, I headed to gate number eight, one of my favorite numbers, and sat down in the waiting area. It was the early nineties, a decade before elaborate security systems were installed. Body scans and pat-downs by smelly security guards weren't yet a concept.

My usual anxiety about air travel was replaced with excitement about seeing Harold.

"I'll be there with bells on." His sweet offer to pick me up at Miami International Airport was readily accepted. (And with three bucks in my wallet; necessary.) It would be our second date, and the first time a gentleman caller would be waiting for me after deplaning. Would he arrive with flowers?

"Eastern Flight 1008 now boarding at gate eight" blared though the PA system and interrupted my daydreaming.

After my carry-on was stowed in the overhead compartment, I nestled into my window seat and finished the coffee I'd shlepped from the Manhattan deli. Despite the caffeine, a sudden wave of exhaustion engulfed me. My eyelids felt heavy while staring out the plane window, challenging my ability to stay awake. The faint murmurs of nearby passengers lulled me into a deep sleep, but it wasn't long before a loud noise, sounding like a train whistle, caught my attention. Outside, on the wing of the plane was a white picket fence. Unsure if we'd taken off or were 20,000 feet above ground, this fence was a confusing sight to behold. A sweet scent wafted through the air and intoxicated me as my eyes fell upon the beautiful magnolia tree situated in the far corner of a manicured front lawn. This sight added more perplexity as the airplane window morphed into a large red door with a welcome mat placed outside an unfamiliar house.

"Come inside," it beckoned.

The red door was alarming. Wasn't red a warning sign for danger? But red was also the universal color for love. My already muddled mind went into overdrive by these conflicting meanings.

Filled with trepidation, I knocked on the door, but no one answered. My hand shook while opening the unlocked door and my breathing labored as I stepped inside.

The living room's huge bay window overlooked a front yard, and the inside furnishings were eclectic. On my right was a dining room set from my parent's home. *How did that get here?*

A tug on my pants leg diverted my attention and a moment later I heard the sweet voice of a child.

"Mommy, when is Daddy gonna be home?"

Mommy? Daddy?

Although there wasn't a logical explanation for my instantaneous familiarity with the child, a maternal bond was felt as I scooped her up in my arms and assured her that Daddy would be home soon. Holding her tightly, peace and contentment swept over me as she tilted her head next to mine. Her soft, silky, yellow hair brushed against my face and my heart swelled.

Off in the distance a train whistle sounded. "The choo choo!" Unable to contain her excitement, she leapt out of my arms and started cleaning up her collection of toys and stuffed animals that had aggregated on the living room floor and sofa. The nightly sound of a train whistle always preceded Harold's arrival. She was a Daddy's girl and she knew he'd frown upon coming home to a mess. (Somehow, this made sense to me, even though I had no idea what was going on.)

The fragrance from the magnolia tree intensified and mixed with the familiar smell of chili con carne cooking on the stovetop.

Harold loved my chili. All of a sudden, I hoped my long-lost brother wouldn't be a vegetarian. Although this situation *felt* very real and normal, I didn't have any recollections about marrying Harold or about how Irving had located me. Try as I might, recalling my wedding day and how I'd reunited with my half sibling was impossible.

Rambling around the living room and opening all the windows allowed the overpowering aromas from outside to squelch my questions. A strange sensation of being inside a poppy field, just like Dorothy in The Wizard of Oz, flashed through my mind. But there wasn't a Tin Man, Scarecrow, or a Cowardly Lion. Just a long-lost brother who'd be on the 5:11 train arriving from Penn Station with Harold, my husband?

While stirring the chili, I felt the familiar touch of my mother's hand on my shoulder and all my questions vanished. "I'm exactly where I'm meant to be," a little voice from inside piped up. A moment later, the soft touch of my mother's gentle hand was replaced by a stranger shaking my shoulder.

"Miss, you'll need to fasten your seatbelt. We're starting our descent." My eyes popped open and watched the flight attendant walk up the aisle. I felt dazed. It took a while to reorient myself to being inside an aircraft instead of a house in the suburbs. By the time the wheels touched the tarmac, writing off the past few hours as a dream wasn't acceptable. That was no dream. Had I been transported through a wormhole to a future reality? Was it too much emotional overload from all the events leading up to this moment in time? Was it just a reaction to last night's bad Chinese food? Could it really be a sign, an omen?

After collecting my carry-on, I exited the plane and felt a newfound calmness within. Approaching the end of the jetway, Harold, holding a bouquet of flowers, came into view. My pace quickened and a minute later we stood in front of each other. His beard hid his smile, but his eyes sparkled.

"Welcome home," he spoke.

A chill coursed through my body and the previous few hours flashed through my mind.

"Just go with it, Rosala," my Mother whispered into my ear.

I returned his smile as he handed me the flowers. The strong magnolia fragrance filled the air.

He took my overstuffed carry-on and extended his other hand. I put my hand in his and our fingers intertwined as we walked through the airport.

"I missed you," we said simultaneously and for the first time in my life, I felt like I was finally home.

Roses' adventures began with the prequel My Life As A Doormat. Not Just My Mother's Daughter, is Rose Gardner's second novel.

My Life as a Doormat follows Rose's life in the 1980's, fresh out of college and moving to Manhattan against her parent's wishes to pursue an acting career. Anxiety-ridden and insecure, Rose fights to maintain her sanity, while establishing herself as an actress and coping with bad relationships, unpredictable roommates, bad decisions, bad jobs, and bad friends.

Here's a preview of *My Life as a Doormat*.

The Arrival

The year was 1980, a time of innocence compared with what would lay ahead. Marijuana was illegal and not available at the corner pharmacy with a doctor's note. The 80's; an era when "cell" referred to miniscule components comprising organic life, or a room in a jail. Cell phones were available but expensive, and used mostly by celebrities who had an entourage to carry them. Terrorist cells were obscure, not on the front page of every newspaper. The horror of 9/11 was in the distant future. Yet, despite the relevant safety of the times, I was terrified.

Here I was, the elevator doors just closed behind me and I dragged my suitcases out to the eighth floor hallway of the building that would be my home. Roberta's distinct raspy voice hurling obscenities at my best friend Ce echoed through out the empty corridor.

"I'm not your friggin bank," Ce screamed back. When Ce had suggested Roberta as a third for our New York City apartment, I was hesitant because I didn't know her very well. Apparently neither did Ce.

My stomach clenched and I heard Mom's words resound inside my head. "Come home Rose!"

"No," I whispered as my mind raced and contemplated her suggestion. "NO!" I repeated. I took a deep breath and tried standing up straight while I pushed down my fear. My roomies screaming at each other like two rivals from a bad soap opera wasn't a sign I should go home. Or was it?

The yelling continued from behind the door of apartment 8A as my grip tightened around the two dilapidated luggage handles. What had happened to make Ce and Roberta sound like they were murdering each other? Sweat beaded on my brow as I heard the elevator doors close behind me.

"It's just 'til next week until my checks clear," Roberta raged.

"That's what you said last week!" I'd never heard Ce in such a state. I felt immobilized but forced my feet to move and shuffled towards the apartment door, dragging my over-stuffed suitcases. Lingering outside the door, I waited until all was quiet.

Silence. What was going on in there? Just as I was about to ring the bell another round of Roberta's diatribe began. My finger froze in mid-air.

"Do I look like Wall Street?" Ce yelled, her shrill scream sent a shiver down my spine.

"I should've stayed in the cab," I whispered to the pale grey carpeting as my body stiffened. Returning to the lobby seemed like a safe alternative to the war zone inside my new home so I parked the two suitcases next to the door and headed back to the elevator bank. But then I froze. *What if I get the unlucky elevator?* Paralyzed with fear, my feet wouldn't move while my eyes darted back and forth from the closed elevator doors to my new residence.

Roberta's voice bounced off the hallway walls while informing Ce she didn't need the lousy apartment.

"FINE!" Ce screamed.

"FINE!" Roberta screamed back.

Five hours earlier I'd been safe and secure in my hometown of Coral Gables, Florida. But now, here I was in an unfamiliar hallway in the giant city of Manhattan, and wondered what the hell was I doing there?

Three months out of college, and much to Mom's dismay, I decided to move to the Big Apple and be an actress. "You're not going to live alone in that filthy, crime-ridden city!"

"I won't be alone. I'm going to share an apartment."

"With who?" Mom opened the oven door, and smoke billowed into the air. "Damn it, Rose, you've got me so upset that I've burnt dinner!" My mother blamed me for everything. "Blame" should've been her middle name, instead of Blanch.

"Sorry," I whispered, and then listened while she laundry listed all of the terrible things I'd done since birth. "Sorry," I repeated and accepted her accusations as absolute truth. She was my mother after all, and I was a respectful child. I stared into space while she removed the charred chicken and placed it on the kitchen counter for her regular scraping ritual.

"With *who*?" she repeated. "Rose! Answer me."

I rolled my eyes, and then left Mom in the kitchen with the burnt bird and soggy vegetables. Every day since graduation we'd had the same argument. I walked into my bedroom, and closed the door. I loved my mother, but hated the worthless way she made me feel.

"Rose!" I heard Mom shriek from the kitchen. I put my hands over my ears and tried muffling the sound of her voice. Was everyone's mother like her, or just mine?

"Get out", I heard Ce scream from inside the apartment and zapped back into reality.

I'd known Ce since kindergarten. Kindergarten; where even at the tender age of six, little girls were bitchy and cliquey. Snotty brats clothed in frilly dresses pulled my hair and laughed at my bleached-out overalls and nautical-themed outfits. All of them; except for Ce. It was the second week of kindergarten when she approached me as I sulked alone in the far corner of the large playroom where daily gymnastics was held (and recess when it rained). While the other kids played checkers and patty-cake, I crouched alone on the far edge of a gym mat, coloring Wilma Flintstone red in a worn coloring book.

"Hi, I'm Chelsea!" The girl with blond pigtails dressed in a pale cornflower-blue dress that matched her eyes kneeled besides me and asked if I wanted to play Chinese checkers

"Sure." Startled, I dropped my crayon as Chelsea led me over to a game next to the popular girls. One of them pointed and warned Chelsea she'd get my cooties as we sat Indian-style across from each other. "I don't know how to play," I blurted out. My eyes welled up while I tried blocking out the popular girls remark. Certain that Chelsea had heard her too and would go back to the clique of kids who already knew how to play games, and wore pretty dresses, I felt invisible.

"That's OK. I'll teach you." Chelsea smiled, and I noticed her two front teeth were missing, just like mine. She reached across the game board and squeezed my hand. "Ill teach you." She repeated. Her smile was reassuring.

"Thanks." For the first time in my short little life I felt validated. From that moment forward we were best friends.

After kindergarten, we went to different elementary schools and my best friend vanished. It wasn't until twelve years later that our paths crossed again.

"I'm in a huge hurry," she'd said the first day of college registration. "Can I cut in front of you?"

Intimidated by the confident stranger with bright blue eyes, blond hair and killer body, I nodded.

"Thanks. I have a plane to catch, and I'm so friggin late!" She sighed then flipped her hair over her shoulder.

"No problem."

"Where ya from?" She asked while the line inched forward at a snail's pace.

"Coral Gables. And you?"

"Miami Beach. I went to Beach High. Where'd you go?"

"Gables."

"You went to Gables?" Her eyes flashed and the beautiful stranger asked if I knew this one and that one. The game of high school who's who was afoot.

Halfway to the registration table, a small flower-shaped gold ring with a tiny red ruby in the middle on her right pinkie caught my attention. "What an unusual ring."

"This?" She rested her hand on her thigh, directly beneath the hem of her micro mini skirt. She claimed it was babyish, and assured me she'd outgrown it. "But I've had it since kindergarten." She smiled. "My dad gave it to me when I was five."

Her ring looked familiar, as if I'd had that exact ring on my finger but couldn't remember when. "I've seen that ring before."

"Yeah?" She looked at her ring, and then studied my face. "My dad had it custom-designed for me," she said and assured me that I must be wrong.

"I remember trying it on," I insisted. "We've met before."

After another round of Florida geography, it was obvious that I'd made a mistake, and my face flushed.

Ce wouldn't give up the game and asked where I'd gone to kindergarten.

"Dearborn."

Ce nodded, yes, she'd gone there too.

"Miss Dundee" with said in unison.

"What's your name?" Ce removed her Foster Grants and stared through me.

"Rose. What's yours?" My shoulders hunched forward as I scanned the ground.

"Ce." She stood up tall and thrust out her chest.

I didn't recognize her name, and shook my head. Another dead-end. A moment later our eyes met and after a long silence, Ce's eyes flashed.

"Rosie Posey! Chinese checkers! Kindergarten! I was Chelsea back then."

"We were best friends," I said with sudden recollection.

"Yes!"

"And you let me wear *that ring*. 'Here ya go, Rosie,' you said. I remember feeling like a princess."

"Next!" Said the registrar behind the table.

After registration we walked outside, and Ce stopped short in the middle of the sidewalk. "Where the hell is it?" she said while rummaging through her purse. "I know I put it in here." A moment later she dumped the contents of her purse onto the pavement.

"What are you looking for?"

"My plane ticket." she muttered and crouched down on bare knees and dug through the large pile. I watched her flailing arms, and sweat pouring down her neck and realized my initial impression of Ce was wrong. She might've looked confidant but wasn't. A confidant peep wouldn't be caught dead on their knees. "Here it is!" she said a few minutes later.

She let out a sigh, but her relief didn't last long. "My flight is tonight, not this afternoon!" she whined. She crumpled the ticket then stuffed it back into her purse, along with the rest of her stuff. "I guess I read the time backward."

"Oh." I stood beside her, smoked a cigarette and tried to hide a smile. I'd found my long lost friend and didn't want to lose her again. "It's a sign," I said, and then helped her to her feet.

"Sign?" Ce put her Foster Grants on and looked like a celebrity.

"Yeah, a sign that we should hang out and catch up." I smiled.

Ce smiled back, and we went for coffee at the Howard Johnson's across the street from campus and picked up where we'd left off twelve years prior. After countless free coffee refills it felt as if we'd never lost touch and I knew that we'd be best friends forever. No matter what.

Once more my best friends voice echoed up and down the hallway. Had her body been invaded by an angry alien? The obscenities she railed at Roberta were uncharacteristic of her docile nature.

During college, most girls kept a cool distance from Ce because they were jealous and felt threatened. With her long, white-blond hair and big, blue eyes, she looked like Goldie Hawn's younger sister. Paper thin, (without the help of an eating disorder) every ounce of her was in the right place; Ce was the Rolls Royce of the female species.

"Here comes the Ice Queen," I'd heard whispered behind Ce's back. Perhaps because I saw her through my kindergarten eyes, I didn't understand those girls' perspective. Ce was the warmest, and best natured person on the planet. Although I felt like my father's Oldsmobile next to her, I couldn't help but be her comrade–in-arms, and in reality, I had no choice.

We were the same person on the inside, but Ce was an excellent actress and faked courage. She exuded confidence while flipping her blond hair over her right shoulder and stood her ground. "Fake it 'til ya make it' she'd tell me. When confronted with adversity I'd panic, obsesses, and devour doughnuts.

Ce helped me overcome my fear about leaving Miami after college graduation. "Rose, you can always come back to Florida to die," she'd

responded to my obsessive worries about leaving my safety net. She wanted
to be a movie star. "If I can't be a movie star, then I want to marry one… or
a millionaire. I have lots of contacts in New York," she assured me.

Wither in Coral Gables, or bloom in the Big Apple? Which was it going
to be? With a roommate like Ce, who'd take me with her to exclusive parties
and all the hot spots in Manhattan, relocating to New York City was too
wonderful to pass up.

Now, three months later, I'd won my independence from my family,
on my own and scared stiff.

Anxiety had squelched exuberance while I'd walked alone through the
airport. I clenched my teeth, and felt more invisible than usual inside the
unfamiliar terminal. My stomach was tied in a gigantic knot as the reality of
being far away from my home set in. I'd lived with my family my entire life,
and even with all of our disagreements and fights, I already missed them.
Especially Mom. And on the long taxi ride to the apartment my mother's
words had replayed in my head. "You can always come home if it doesn't
work out, Rose. I won't change a thing in your room." Mom's cheeks drew
inward as she inhaled on her cigarette. What confidence she had in me.

"How will you survive in that cold weather?" she had asked daily.
"You have Florida blood for God's sake!"

But fall in New York was spectacular, and none of my mom's fears
would keep me from opening the door to my future.

Roberta's shrieking refocused my thinking.

"No money: NO apartment; GOT IT?" I heard Ce, the wannabe
millionaire movie queen screech back at Roberta.

Roberta. She was the second roommate, and the complete opposite of
Ce and me. Also a drama major at the University of Miami, Roberta was
more interested in engineering spotlights than being in one. She designed
light boards, built sets, wore overalls and got her hands dirty. The set crews

for our college theater productions called her "Bert." She seemed pretty mellow and was the theatrical equivalent of Wonder Bread. Although Ce and I didn't know her well when she expressed an interest in moving to New York City, we decided she would bring the perfect balance to our apartment. Besides, she needed a place to live and had the finances to move to Manhattan, or so we thought. We never suspected her to be a pathological liar with unsavory motives and hidden agendas. Never.

"Oh go to hell!" Ce screamed again, louder then before.

Roberta mumbled something unintelligible, and the sound of broken glass followed. No longer immobilized, I took several more steps towards the elevator bank.

"This is just not going to work out." Ce's rebuttal to Roberta's unintelligible comments was deafening.

I stared at the thin black and gray stripes on the wallpaper in the empty hallway and fought the urge to count them. Flashbacks flooded my mind about my first visit to New York City. "I can't live here! The buildings are too tall!"

"Don't worry, Rose. They won't fall on you," Ce had joked.

I had faked a smile but had wanted to back out of our great New York adventure.

"Rose you are making a huge mistake!" Mom's parting words at Miami International Airport repeated over and over. Maybe she was right after all.

I'd been living life guided by Carole King and Carly Simon song lyrics and now, at last, the journey that would confirm or deny all the things I'd only heard about through their music had begun. "Tonight you're mine, completely, you give your love so sweetly." I wouldn't be answering to my mother anymore, or listening to my dad's insanity. I'd stay out all night drinking French wine with interesting men in secluded bistros. We'd French kiss in the backseat of a cab while it sped up the avenue en route to their cozy apartment. "But will you love me tomorrow?"

"No I'm not going back to Coral Gables!" I said out loud.

The elevator doors opened but no one got out. As I stared at the empty elevator I realized it was the lucky one, as if it had come back for me.

"I only ride on lucky elevator number one." I informed my mom when I was nine years old. She had rolled her eyes, believing that some day I'd grow out of this odd behavior. But I didn't.

I can just turn around, walk through those lucky doors, and go home. Hail a cab to the airport and go back to Coral Gables. But a stronger urge stopped me from running away. I had dreamt of this moment. Real life was about to start. Excitement replaced fear and I whispered, "Free at last. Free at last" and heard the lucky elevator's doors close.

Backing away from the elevator bank, I returned to the apartment door and stood beside my two brown suitcases, which held everything I thought I would need to make a start in this strange, exciting city. There was silence on the other side of the apartment door, so I held my breath and rang the bell.

Cue The Girl
(a year, and several roommate's later)

The next day, I waited all afternoon for Ethan's return from the hospital. Posed on the couch, dressed in my tightest jeans and a low-cut white silk blouse (borrowed from Ce's closet), the minutes dragged on like hours. Finally, around four o'clock, I heard his key in the front door while I pretended to flip through a *Cosmo* magazine and tried to be nonchalant. A moment later, the sound of the door opening sent a shiver up my spine. My face felt flushed, and my heart was racing with heated anticipation. I buried my face in the magazine after the door shut, and I heard Ethan's footsteps as he walked into the living room. "Hi." My voice squeaked while I tried to act cool as Ethan breezed by.

"Hey," he said, keeping his eyes glued to the floor while he headed to his bedroom, then shut the door.

My heart sank. "I'm such a fool!" I whispered, realizing that a reprise of yesterday's make-out session wasn't on Ethan's agenda. He remained sequestered inside his room while I lingered on the couch and hoped for at least an acknowledgement of what had transpired the previous day.

Forty minutes later, Ethan re-emerged. "I'm off to the library." He walked past me and hid his face behind a tall stack of books he carried between his outstretched arms.

"Oh." All hopes of a love connection disintegrated and I was crushed.

"Rose?" Ethan said after he'd crossed the living room.

"Yes?" I snapped to and bolted upright. Perhaps I'd given up hope a little too soon. Maybe, he was just taking his time. Or maybe…

"Would ya grab the door for me?"

"Sure." I dragged my feet across the living room floor and opened the door.

"Later, Rose."

Ethan left without a backwards glance. I watched him get into elevator number 2 and heard the faint sounds of the elevator doors closing. "Later Ethan," I said to the empty hallway then slammed the door.

After that afternoon, he was never around. He'd become the invisible roommate, and any hopes of a romance with Ethan Schwartz faded.

By the end of the month, I was done with men (especially Ethan, and any men referred by him) and focused on my lack of a career. I went to hundreds of casting calls listed in the trade papers (along with thousands of other actors). Off Broadway didn't want me, so I tried Off Off Broadway productions and never got cast in those, either. (Occasionally, I'd get callbacks for plays located so far off Broadway they were in Staten Island. Or Queens.) Through wind, rain, sleet and hail, I schlepped to auditions feeling empathy for postal workers. At least they were paid for braving the elements. With the subway fares, acting classes, headshots, and missed waitress shifts, pursuing my acting career was costing me a shitload of cash.

The open calls for extra work in films, unlike the try-outs for stage, didn't require an audition, only hours of waiting in line to hand in my headshot.

"Here you go," I'd say to a production assistant while handing her my slightly retouched 8-by-10 photo, which she would throw on top of hundreds of others. Sometimes I'd get lucky. Many films, especially those directed by Woody Alan, used Manhattan and me as a backdrop. I had stepped up from unemployed actor to "extra," working in the background on one film after another.

The first time I earned a part in a film, I was ecstatic and couldn't wait to call Pam.

"I got some work on a Woody Allen film," I told her.

"That's nice." Her voice was low, and she sounded like she had a horrible cold. Or was crying. "Just make sure ya don't talk to Woody Allen unless he talks to you; otherwise you'll get fired." She sniffed.

"Whaddya mean?"

"He's a weirdo. Trust me on this, Rose. I'll call you later, 'cause I'm kinda busy right now." She explained that she was in the middle of a fight with her boyfriend, a podiatrist, and then hung up the phone.

"That's nice?" Pam's response was a letdown. I needed to share my fantastic news with someone who'd be as ecstatic as I was, so I called my mom.

"Mom's not here," Heather answered the phone and was charming as ever.

"Heather, I got a part in a movie!" I should've known better, but the words just slipped out.

"How many lines do ya have?" she snipped, sounding annoyed.

"Uh, well… none… I'm just an extra, and Woody Allen is directing!"

"Who's Woody Allen? How much money are ya gonna make?"

"Not much, but that's not the point…"

"You're never gonna be a real actress. Ever. Why don't you give up and just get a real job like everybody else?"

I couldn't answer as my tears welled up and stung my eyes.

"I'll tell Mom you called." I could see her smirking on the other end of the phone line and felt a hot tear on my cheek. "Gotta go."

After my tenth extra job, Heather's blasé reaction (minus the bitchiness) became my own. Granted, I was on a roll with getting film gigs. But the roll I was on wasn't soft or delicious like a plump Kaiser available from any Lower East Side deli. My role was more like a piece of three-day-old stale bread from Mikos. Working as an extra wasn't consistent with my visions of a thriving acting career, let alone stardom.

"Cue the girl," I'd hear the production assistant say while he motioned for me to walk from point A to point B as someone yelled "picture up" followed by "rolling." What next? Maybe I'd be asked to skip, hop or even limp. Nope. Walk. I bet if I had bigger boobs someone would ask me to skip. If I had really, really big boobs, perhaps someone would put me in an aerial harness and fly me across the friggin' bloody set. Director after director appeared oblivious to my immense talent and capabilities. Couldn't they see that sticking me in the background while the stars recited their lines was a complete waste of my dramatic aptitude?

July arrived, and I'd at last I was a member of The Screen Actors Guild.

"That is so great!" Ethan sounded warm and genuine. "I'm happy for you" he said and handed me July's rent check. "Now you're a professional extra."

"Background artist," I said, trying to impress him, even though I knew I was like mobile furniture on the set. Ethan's word "extra" made me feel invisible and insignificant. Ethan having a steady girlfriend added salt to the wound. She was a nurse at the hospital who he'd been dating casually, but then it got serious right after our passionate encounter. Her name was Judith, and she was the reason Ethan had become the invisible roommate. Even though I'd never met Nurse Judith, I hated her. Ethan slept at her place every night and never hung out at our apartment anymore. He used his room as a storage unit, or a refuge for when they'd had a fight. That was fine. The less I saw of him, the better, I tried convincing myself. I came to New York City to be an actress, and that was my primary focus.

Fed up with feeling like a robotic piece of meat, I decided to decline all parts without dialogue. I'd been in Manhattan almost a year, and I was through being a professional extra. Absolutely, completely done without exception — until the next call came.

"You'll be playing a secretary," the casting director said. "So whatever you do, Rose, don't wear jeans."

My ears perked up. Playing? "Is it a speaking role?"

"Not this time, but I promise to keep you in mind for anything I think you'd be right for."

I knew she was lying. She knew she was lying. But I was broke and jobless 'cause Mikos had to shut down after failing a health inspection. My vow to refuse extra work was about to be broken. "Thank you." I took a big bite of my stale pride sandwich and accepted the gig.

Half asleep and chugging coffee, I rode the subway at five-thirty in the morning to the location site. Carole King's lyrics to "Beautiful" resounded in my head as I noticed the other passengers.

You've got to get up every morning with a smile on your face.

The crowd on this subway car had never heard that song. Would I ever be traveling to a film location via limo instead of on the smelly No. 6 train? Carole's words continued haunting me.

People gonna treat you better, you're gonna find, yes you will, that you're as beautiful as you feel.

Yeah, right.

Twenty minutes later, with just one small coffee spill on my shirtsleeve, I checked in with the production assistant.

"Hi, Rose," said the girl, who at first glance looked like a guy. She looked familiar, and then her flannel plaid shirt jogged my memory.

"Roberta?"

"How ya been?" She glanced up from the piece of paper containing a list of names. The same nondescript hairstyle and expressionless brown eyes confirmed it was she.

"Great," I lied, remembering the hole she'd left in the wall of my apartment, the hole that had never been repaired.

"How's Ce?" Roberta asked.

"Ce? Oh, she's great. She's a shoe model now. And in Japan for the summer."

"Figures," Roberta said in a monotone voice. She gave me a number then directed me to a room full of other women all dressed up for a day of playing secretary at the office.

I filled out the paperwork. Line two: Dependents. Dependents? I couldn't remember what to fill in there, so I just put down my lucky number: 10. I took a few seconds to study my role, which was labeled No. 45.

Familiar with the hurry-up-and-wait routine of the background artist business, I pretended to read a book while checking out the crowd. All types of people were here, and I knew the production crew was adhering to the casting rules regarding minorities. We were all represented; the young and the old, the Asian, African-American, Native American Indian, Spanish, and a few Jews among the WASPs. We were a big blended family sitting together in a large room with a funny smell. What if there's a gas leak? Or something worse.

"Big deal." Heather's mocking voice drummed inside my head. "Isn't being poisoned just a small price to pay for a second or two of fame?"

I ignored her imaginary comments, and the smell, while my eyes focused on a group of women in there forties instead. "That's never gonna be me," I whispered while I eavesdropped on their game of one-up-man-ship

I heard the overweight, bleached-blond actress pushing fifty claiming it was between her and Goldie Hawn for the part in 'Private Benjamin'.

"I was almost in the film version of 'Sister Act,' but the director thought I looked too much like Whoopi," another wannabe chimed in.

Another nobody touted how it was between her and Bernadette Peters for the lead role in 'Into The Woods'. If these celebrities in their own minds were on the verge of stardom, then what the hell were they doing here? It was times like these when I missed Ce the most and wondered what time it was in Japan. If she'd been with me, we would've laughed together while trashing these women to bits.

"I'll only accept background work until I'm thirty, and if I'm not a star by then." I'd say.

…"I'll consider leaving New York and going to law school," Ce would've finished my sentence. Now all I had to listen to was the irritating voices of all these wannabes and the memory of my mother's last phone call.

"Rose, you can always come home if New York isn't working out. No one will think you're a failure," Mom said, showing deep confidence in my talents. "If you went to law school, then you could get a real job, with health benefits. Isn't being a lawyer just like acting? You might even meet someone and get married." A husband for me and a son-in-law for her was what she wanted, not a daughter waiting tables and checking coats while chasing a dream. "I deserve some happiness," she'd say, and then remind me that all of her friends' daughters were married. All her friends had well-off sons-in-law and bragged about their grandchildren. "I'll send you Elaine Feldman's wedding announcement, a full-pager in the Sunday Miami Herald."

"Please don't." Elaine and I hadn't spoken in years. And besides, who friggin cared!

"Well, just give law school a thought," Mom persisted; thinking maternal hocking could be effective.

"I'll think about it," was my standard less-than-true closing remark each time I'd hang up the phone, doubt my choices and wonder what was to become of me.

"I need numbers twenty-eight, twenty-nine, and forty-five," Roberta boomed in a loud voice, bringing me back to reality. "Let's go, people, they're ready to shoot the scene." I followed my ex-roommate to an elevator bank.

"Bye, Rose," Roberta said, leaving us all to pile into the middle elevator. I was disappointed that lucky No. 1 hadn't shown up but settled for the neutrality of No. 2. "Bye Roberta," I yelled back as the elevator doors closed.

We rode up to the fifteenth floor in silence. The short African-American girl in her twenties (No. 28) stared straight ahead while No. 29 (a beautiful Asian woman pushing forty) dug around in her purse. And I held my breath. As usual, the ride seemed endless, and I was relived when the elevator doors opened.

A man holding a walkie-talkie escorted us to the set, an office containing three desks. He sprinted out and now the assistant director was in charge. He told the Asian woman to sit behind the first desk and instructed her to type. The African-American girl was picked next and placed behind the third desk.

"Thumb through some papers and look busy," the assistant director told her. "Number forty-five, go sit at the desk in the middle."

I raced over and sat down behind the desk. "What do you want me to do?"

The assistant director thought for a moment. "Say 'Good morning' as Michael passes by your desk."

"You want me to speak?" I asked dumbfounded that fate had at long last twisted its head in my direction.

"Yeah, do ya have a problem with that?" the assistant director answered then walked away.

Did I have a problem with that? Was he kidding? I was on cloud nine and wished I could call Ethan and tell him the news. Perhaps he'd be so impressed he'd dump the nurse and realize he wanted to be with an aspiring star instead. Now that I had a speaking part on camera, I felt confident my career was on the upswing. A few moments later, still stunned, I rehearsed my line with the assistant director as the other two background artists shot green daggers at me out of their eyes. Their evil glare didn't faze me; it enhanced my performance.

"Good morning," I said, over and over again tilting my head this way and that. Yes, I was ready for my close-up, Mr. De Mille, and had been for years. This was long overdue, and if anyone thought they were going to rain on my parade, they could just forget it! Especially the two ethnically diverse clones sitting behind me.

Ten minutes later, the star of the movie sauntered in. He'd been working out in his Winnebago with his trainer from Body by Jake. He stubbed out his cigarette as the assistant director told him we'd rehearse once and then yelled "roll tape."

"Scene eighteen, take one and action," I heard as the young star dressed in a suit walked in front of the three desks and stopped for a moment to be greeted by my "Good morning" monologue. The whole experience was surreal, yet it was happening. I was speaking after working in all those films where my roles were as silent as Greta Garbo's earliest on-screen appearances. We rehearsed and shot the scene. And then the party was over.

There was a flurry of activity as the director of the movie rushed in. "Sorry I'm late. I had to take a call from the coast," he said in a loud, Brooklyn accent.

"No problem." The assistant director told him. I overheard the AD assure Mr. Director that we'd rehearsed and already had one take in the can. The director looked over in my direction, checking our secretarial pool of three. The star in the suit stepped out for another smoke.

"Who's the girl in the middle? The one wearing the purple jacket?" I thought I was going to faint as Mr. Director pointed at me. Was I being discovered? Was it this easy? I felt my heart pounding, ready to leap out of my chest. I held my breath and eavesdropped some more on the conversation held less than six feet away from my desk.

"She's the secretary who greets Michael when he makes his entrance," answered the assistant director.

I felt the director's eyes staring through me as he said, "Well, she doesn't fit in with the other girls, so replace her, but keep the jacket so we can match the shot."

What happened? I was now starring in a horror film playing in my head. Doesn't fit in? What did that mean? I sat frozen behind the desk, and pretended as if I hadn't heard the conversation that was audible to everyone on the set. The two other secretaries, with whom I didn't "fit in," wore vicious grins as the assistant director came over and told me there'd been a change in the scene and my acting talents were no longer needed. I was being replaced.

Bewildered and afraid that if I got up out of the chair I'd break just like a piece of fragile glass, I felt tears begin to well up. Somehow I managed to disappear off the set, find the closest bathroom, and throw up. Between the tears and the vomit, I wasn't a pretty sight. Maybe law school wasn't such a bad idea after all.

The words to "Beautiful" started playing in my head again. This time I tuned them out and told them to screw off. It took half an hour to gain enough composure to exit the lady's room. Waiting by the bathroom door was the assistant director. Was he waiting for me? Had they changed their minds? Was I being reinstated? I looked like hell, but I could apply fresh make-up and be ready to go back on the set in ten minutes. After all, I was a trooper. My standard fantasy was abruptly interrupted.

"Uh," the assistant director looked a bit uncomfortable as he asked, "Could we borrow your purple jacket? The director liked the color."

Trance-like, I handed him my jacket so my replacement could wear it — my replacement, who would be saying my line while wearing my jacket. I felt pleasure knowing I'd used the inside of my coat as a large handkerchief to wipe away the tears and clean the vomit that had adorned my face just minutes before. If I was being robbed of my one second of fame, and the thieves wanted to use my jacket, my replacement would just have to deal with it. Of course, I made no mention of this information. To this day, I hate the color purple.

If you've enjoyed these excerpts from **My Life as a Doormat***, the complete novel can be ordered from:*

thesocietyforrecoveringdoormats.com
(USA only) or obtained worldwide through AMAZON.

Praise for **My Life as a Doormat**

Every woman will identify with Rose and her struggles and will be inspired by the way Rose overcomes crippling self-doubt. I want to take Rose out for coffee and thank her for showing me how to find confidence.

Terena Scott, Publisher, Medusa's Muse Press

*   *   *   *   *

Rose Gardner has a knack for reaching in and grabbing your heart. We all have friends like Rose, or we're related to her, and in many instances, we are Rose. We all dream the same dreams of success, romance and happiness. But life doesn't always cooperate, and *My Life as a Doormat* exemplifies this through the lens of the millions of people who suffer, like Rose, from low self-esteem.

Rose soulfully demonstrates the heart-breaking vulnerabilities of a doormat personality, as well as the triumphs of life as a recovering doormat. Her humor and generous spirit allow us to gently examine our own behaviors and invite healing.

Dr. Terry Segal, Ph.D. in Energy Medicine, Licensed Psychotherapist
Author of *The Enchanted Journey: Finding the Key that Unlocks You and Hidden Corners of My Heart*.

Praise for The Society for Recovering Doormats

"Congratulations for connecting with over 256,000 individuals. To be a Doormat would imply feeling inferior, unworthy, to be passive, never express yourself, and to be a victim. To be a Recovering Doormat would imply feeling a sense of personal worth, that you have rights, that your voice is meant to share your core values, and that you connect with others. In this case 256,000 and growing. Congratulations for being the conduit, the portal, and the vehicle that so many relate to and identify with. Keep making a difference."

- Dr, Harold Shinitzky, practicing psychologist, former President of Florida Psychological Association and Recipient of the 2022 Distinguished Service Award. Author of *A Champion's Mindset: 15 Mental Conditioning Steps to Becoming a Champion Athlete.*

You can check out the society public Facebook page at *The Society for Recovering Doormats* **and at the members only site at** *thesocietyforrecoveringdoormats.com.*

www.ingramcontent.com/pod-product-compliance
Lightning Source LLC
Chambersburg PA
CBHW021459250626
47154CB00004BA/1609